JOHN PASCAL

*Now choose life so that you and your
children may live, and that you may love
the Lord your God, listen to His voice
and hold fast to Him. DT 30: 19-20*

MY CHILD

September 2016. Revised August 2025

ISBN# 13: 978-0-692-78824-0

      10: 0- 692-78824-7

Copyright pending

John Pascal Books

Bible quotations from "The New International Version," Copyright 1984, Zondervan Corp.

NOTE: MY CHILD tells a story that stands alone. However, it is also a sequel to WINGIN' IT, so the reader will enjoy a fuller appreciation of the characters, both human and some angel friends of theirs, by reading that story first.

PRELUDE

The dancers squirmed around each other, hands upraised, swaying to the laser lights and a throbbing musical beat. Jasmine Tynan was clumsy as she attempted to keep up with Derek. He was dancing with her, and also with another woman who had moved in on them.

She stood on tiptoe to shout in his ear. "Do they have anything to eat at this nightclub? I'm getting weak."

"But Jill's trying to teach us a cool new step."

Jill turned to face Jasmine but continued dancing, arms raised, body still undulating. She laughed. "Derry-Derry, with this one you brought in, I think *every* step is new."

Jasmine kept her focus on the ear. "Please?"

Derek tossed his head back, then looked down at his date, her red hair full of sparkling confetti, her eyes full of desperation. "Sure, Jazzy." Dancing closer to Jill, he pointed. "Bartender on that end has some food. Tell him 'Marston tab.' Have anything you want. Be there in a bit."

Jasmine nodded, gave him an air kiss, and turned away, but she made sure Jill caught her warning scowl. She worked her way through the dancers, twice shocked by the hands groping her as she passed.

It was a good fifteen minutes and several propositions later, three by men and one by a woman, before Derek found her at the end of the bar, cowering against a wall. "Hey, hi babe. Hope you got something to eat. This nightlife's a little new for ya, huh?"

She looked up with wide, searching eyes, but smiled bravely. "I had two egg rolls and half a 'Bartender's Special' brownie. It tasted weird. I'm just a county girl, I guess."

Derek gun-pointed at the bartender. "Dewar's and a champagne." He grinned at Jasmine. "Sorry, but we've been going out for months now, and I was getting tired of just dinner and a good night kiss. I know you spent most of your life in a wheelchair. Time to have more fun, don't you think?"

She put her hand on his shoulder. "If you like to come here once in a while, I'm sure I'll get used to it, Darling. Jill called you Derry-Derry?"

Derek took the drinks from the bartender and handed her the champagne. "Jill? She's a fixture around this club— got a pet name for everyone."

"I think I have a name for her, too." She grabbed the edge of the bar.

"Say, you look a little woozy, Jazzy."

"I am. Must be the bubbles. Is there anywhere to sit?"

He chuckled. "Actually, it's the special brownie." He put an arm around her waist. "Come on, sweets. They have an outside place with tables."

Jasmine slumped into an iron patio chair, too trembly to hold the glass one-handed. "It's cooler out here." She shook her head and exhaled. "I'm sure I'll be okay in a minute."

"Ahh, you'll be fine. Look, I know this has been a bit much for you, and you've never been to my place. Maybe for once we should go there and relax."

"But, you know I…uh, Christian girls don't go to men's apartments."

"Ahh, but this is different, Jazzy. We're *special* now. Time we engage in more than conversation."

"Engage? Engage in what?"

He chuckled. "Better things. Besides, I've got something important I want to tell you, and it has to be in private." He leaned in toward her ear and whispered. "It's about us."

"But I shouldn't. I…" She grinned. "You're not hinting at a *proposal*, are you, Derek?"

A thin smile came over his face as he moved in close to her wide, clouded eyes. "You *know* I love you, babe, but you'll just have to come and see. Finish that champagne up like a good girl, and let's go."

ONE

The next day, Nurse Tynan pushed her cart into the pediatric ward, humming "Make Someone Love You." Her nurse's cap floated on top of her fluffy red curls. Caps weren't required anymore, but she liked them. She poured two little cups of medicine, put on a big smile, and walked over to the patient who was scowling at her from the corner bed.

An eight-year-old girl stared into her nurse's eyes with folded arms, her face in full pout. Jasmine leaned over, squinted, and smiled at her defiance. "Now, Mindy, you know you *have* to take your medicine. You don't want that leg bone infection to come back, do you? Remember how it hurt?"

"Leg's all better now!" She pointed at the white cup being held out to her. "And *that* stuff tastes yucky."

"So, you've forgotten all about that leg pain, huh?" Jasmine bent down to her eye level. "Hmmm." She sniffed at the cup in her hand. "Smells good to me, Mindy. It's banana flavor, and I know you like them."

"That's no banana."

Jasmine laughed. "That is true, my dear, but Doctor Marston says you have to be on this for ten days or those germs inside might grow back and start hurting you again. Worse than that, your broken bone won't heal. You want to stay here another week and go back on the IV?"

Mindy shook her head. "He's a grumpy old doctor."

Jasmine straightened up and pouted back with hands on her hips. "Nonsense. He's our handsome chief Orthopedic Resident and Doctor Wright's consultant. Besides, I happen to know he can be nice, too." She held up a hand and pretended to be giving an injection. "I'm the mean one."

Tears began to slide down Mindy's red cheeks. Jasmine put the cup down and sat on the edge of the bed. She picked up her little hand, took a tissue from the bedside stand, and patted her cheek.

Jasmine's voice became low and soft. "Look, I know. How about this, Mindy? You take a small sip of the yummy cherry one first, then gulp all the banana down real quick and finish the cherry. Then you'll just taste the cherry. I promise."

Mindy was still frowning, but she nodded. The plan worked, and Jasmine patted her head. "Good girl."

"Why are you happy today, Nurse Tynan?"

"And what makes you think I'm so happy?"

"I saw you singing and swinging around over there."

"Well, I'll be," she giggled. "Very observant, little one."

"What's ob-ser-vant?"

"It means you're smart and pay attention. Okay, because you've been so good today, I'll tell you, but you can't tell *anyone*—not one soul. Word of honor?"

A wide-eyed grin came over Mindy's face. "It's a real *secret*?"

"Yes, and it will be *just* between us. Promise?"

Mindy nodded with vigor. "Oh yes, I *promise*."

Jasmine slid closer to her and dropped her voice. "I think Doctor Marston is going to ask me to marry him tomorrow."

Mindy frowned and shook her head. "Marry grumpy doctor? You *like* him?" She looked over Jasmine's head and grinned at the tall man standing behind her. "Hi, Doctor Wright. Not a good idea, is it?"

Jasmine jumped up, hand over her mouth. "Oh, Doctor Wright, I didn't know you were there."

"Sorry to surprise you, but I couldn't help but watch your masterful handling of my difficult patient. I'd give you an A plus on bedside manner, but I'll have to agree with Mindy and give you a D minus on your choice of men."

"Oh yeah? What would you know about that?" Jasmine marched back to her cart. "I've taken your advice on other things, Sam, but you're a *man* and this is something only a woman would understand."

Sam chuckled. "Even if she's only eight."

TWO

Doctor Stephen Schwartz entered his house through the garage entrance, briefcase in hand. "Hi Honey, I'm back."

A distant whisper-voice replied. "David's room. Don't shout."

Stephen inhaled a whiff of Italian cooking with a smile, put his case down, and made his way upstairs. Paula sat in a powder blue room rocking and nursing her baby in the waning light from the window behind her. Her congenitally short left arm was just sufficient to hold her baby's head against her while he enjoyed dinner.

Exaggerating a quiet walk, Stephen swayed up to them and whispered. "Didn't think it was possible, but you're even more beautiful today."

Paula looked up with a grin. "So glad you've conquered your old habit of saying the wrong thing." She sent him an air smooch.

He bent down to have a close look at his boy. He whispered with mock sternness: "Uh oh, David, you found those in Daddy's toy box, didn't you?"

Paula snorted. "Stop it, you. I can't laugh right now. Sit down and tell me about your day."

Stephen kissed her forehead and pulled a chair over. "Where should I start?"

"How about the first thing that's on your mind?"

"Okay. Is that spaghetti sauce I smell?"

Paula's chest thumped with a suppressed laugh. "Quit it, silly. David's almost asleep. Don't spoil it."

"Well, I thought that was a very serious question."

"It's sauce for the lasagna. Anything else besides food and breasts inside that male brain of yours?"

Stephen laughed. "Well, David started it." He stared up at the ceiling and gritted his teeth in thought. "No, don't think so—wait, *football!*" He grinned. "There's a Broncos game on tonight."

Paula stuck out her tongue.

Raising his hands, "Oh, I get it. You mean my day at *work.*"

Her eyes glistening with mirth, she shook her head. "Sure, why don't you give *that* a try?"

"Okay, I'll get serious." He scooted his chair closer. "That teenage boy you know, James from your painting class? His CP is worse, and he's been falling with just the cane he's been using. He hurt his hand and we moved him to a walker."

"Oh, pooh. I thought he was stable. James is a real artist. How bad is the hand?"

"Sprained wrist. Nothing broken, and he said he'd still be in your class this weekend."

"That's good. He's been doing impressionist works like he invented the style all on his own. In a year, he'll have enough finished work to enter a judging at the museum."

"And there's Susan Spencer, who works next to you at Genomics. She'll be out at least two weeks with pneumonia, and that means they'll use temps and have only one person with telephone experience until you get back."

"Nothing like job security." Paula got up slowly and whispered, "Put the crib rail down, will you? He's asleep now."

"Ah, if that would only last the night."

"Yup, and you're first up for the diaper change." Paula placed her baby on his side in the crib, covered him, and gently raised the rail. "I think we're good for a few hours." She embraced Stephen so they could exchange a proper welcome-home kiss.

Downstairs, Stephen lifted the cover on the bubbling sauce to enjoy the aroma. "There's something else I want to talk to you about, but first I need to get my slippers on and a glass of Barbera in my hand."

"Sure, Steve, but while you're in the kitchen, could you give the pot a stir and turn the heat to low?"

Settling into the living room couch, Paula curled her legs up and embraced the Perrier and cranberry Stephen fixed for her. "So, what's up?"

"I was at the hospital talking with doctor Sam Wright from Mountain Medical Group. Don't think you've met him, but he's a real nice guy."

"Jazzy's said nice things about him, but isn't he your competition?"

"Doesn't work that way in medicine. She's known him since her early wheelchair days, maybe nine or ten years. Anyway, he was part of the orientation team assigned to Jazzy when she was hired last year, and they've continued to be friends."

"Dating?"

"No, no. Didn't you know? She's been seeing an orthopedic resident for the past few months. She and Sam are just friends, but she respects him—one of the few who dares to give her advice."

"Oh, good. I think she's tired of listening to my two cents all the time. Still, I'm hurt she never told me about this special boyfriend. Think there's a problem?"

"Hopefully not, but it's been over a year since Jazzy's miraculous healing, and, as you know, she's been like a young colt released into pasture."

Paula flopped her head back on the cushion. "Oh, I *know*. Suddenly, there she is: a pretty, young woman with a sparkling personality and walking free. No wonder all the men are after her. Unfortunately, Jasmine hasn't dated since high school and has no idea how immature she is socially. Even worse, her idea of men is like some idealized teenage memory."

She turned to her husband. "But, last time we talked, Jazzy assured me she's been a good Christian girl and careful, so what's this all about?"

"Sam has warned her about this man she has a crush on, this Derek Marston. He tells me the guy is a real womanizer with a string of broken hearts in his wake."

"Nerts. And lemme guess. She just laughs off Sam's advice."

"Right on."

"Jazzy never even *mentioned* Derek to me, and I'm her best friend. What does that tell you?"

"That it could be worse than I thought."

THREE

Sunday afternoon, Jasmine floated along the path in the park, the sweet smell of spring expanding her exuberance. Every flower from callalilies to dandelion tops seemed to have become a magnificent work of art in her eyes, and all the birds sang songs of love.

A mallard and his mate swam toward her as she walked on the path beside the lake. She stopped for a moment to watch them swimming together, put her hands on her hips, and spoke out loud: "I know what *you* two are up to." She laughed.

She touched her head to adjust her nurse's cap, thought better of it, stuffed the cap in her bag, and thought: *He's going to want to take me out to lunch after he proposes, and I didn't even think to fix myself up.*

Jasmine whisked a comb through her wavy red hair and tried to resume a more casual pace to her rendezvous, but when she saw him on the bench, she skipped over, slid in next to him, and planted a quick kiss on his cheek.

"There you are, Derek, darling. Isn't this just a *glorious* day the Lord has made? And what a perfect spot you picked for us to meet."

Derek patted her hand and made furtive eye contact. "You certainly look cheerful." He swallowed a bite in his mouth and crumpled a brown bag beside him.

Jasmine snuggled closer and grinned. "You seem a bit nervous, but I understand. Who *wouldn't* be, but I won't be pushy." She gazed upon his face, her blue eyes wide and filled with a lifetime of hope. "All right, Derek, you said you had something very *important* to tell me."

"Uh, yeah. I'm taking a position in Tucson with the leading Orthopedic Group there. They've offered me a full partnership in just *one* year. Can you believe it? Much better deal than anything around here."

"Oh, Derek," She took his hand and pressed it to her chest. "*That's* why you're upset. You think I'd hate to leave my friends, my job, and all. Sweetheart, I want you to know that you and your career are all that's important to me now. I'll be *completely* happy in Tucson as long as I'm with you, darling."

"But, I—you don't…"

Jasmine still held his hand and moved it to his leg with deliberation. She grinned, patted it in place, and straightened up with a big breath. "All right, just relax. I'll be quiet. I understand that telling me at your place was the inappropriate moment. So now, go ahead and tell me about this important something."

Derek turned, this time making eye contact. "Jasmine, that was *it*. I'm moving away, and I knew this would upsct you. I didn't want to spoil our party night and the good time we were having. But you seem to have some crazy idea about us, don't you?"

For a moment, Jasmine just stared into his eyes, searching for meaning. "You—baa-blu..." Words were not forming. "You're not proposing?"

Derek shuddered. "Proposing? No, why would you think that?"

Jasmine's hand went to her mouth, and her voice became hoarse. "Saturday night. After the party, I went to your apartment for the first time 'cause you said we were 'engaged to be engaged.' You said you'd have something very important to tell me real soon—and you *winked*."

He chuckled. "Who *knows* what I said Friday night? I was pretty plastered, and you were full of champagne too."

Jasmine jumped up to face him. "Cause you kept *asking* me to keep drinking until I passed out. Derek, I gave you what I shouldn't have—what a woman can only give a man *once*."

"And you should be proud." He chuckled. "You might be the most 'hard-to-get' girl I've ever met, but you were really *something* Friday night. *That* I do remember."

"Ahh," she squealed, a 'bomb' exploding in her head. "You don't love me at *all*!"

"Not true, babe." He grinned. "Not true at all. You're one great gal, and I'll be back in Denver once in a while. My sister lives here. And listen, you could come and visit me in 'AZ', too. We'll still hook up some."

Jasmine kicked at his foot, and they stared at each other in silence. The anger on her face drained, and her jaw became slack. She got up and briskly walked away.

He called to her back. "Hey, I'll phone you when I'm set up there. Promise."

Jasmine headed for her car outside the park, her pace quickening as an agonizing panic overcame her. She almost made it to the street, but turned to lean against a tree when the dry heaves began.

FOUR

Stephen sat in his little office munching Paula's hero sandwich while he typed on the computer. Doctor Anderson appeared in his doorway with a tap-tap on the frame. "Got a sec, Steve? Sorry to bother you at lunch."

"Not at all." He waved him in but kept his index finger raised until he finished typing the sentence. "What's up, boss?"

Anderson was wheezing loudly but he took a few strides in and sat in a chair by the desk. "Not boss for long, Steve." Wheeze. "You'll be a partner when I retire in two months and I'll bet you'll be running this practice in a couple of years."

Stephen chuckled. "Now there's a scary thought, John."

"I'm concerned about a patient we share." Anderson took a few musical breaths through his ruddy cheeks. "Our miracle woman…"

"Jasmine?"

"Yes, paralyzed since teenage. The one who couldn't *possibly* be walking and now graces our hospital with song and dance. She's your wife's best friend, I think." Another wheezy breath. "And I think I'll take my own advice and change my asthma medication tomorrow."

"My advice too, John. But what's up with Jazzy?"

John chuckled. "Cute name. Well, as you know she's been healthy as a race horse and spreading cheer wherever she goes."

"Yeah, she even did a ballet number for the Christmas show on the children's ward. But say, when God gives you back your legs why not flaunt them?"

"She called in sick yesterday afternoon—said she had the stomach flu and I wrote her an excuse sight unseen, but she was going to come in for a checkup today."

"Yeah, that virus is going around, and she works with sick kids every day."

Anderson began coughing. He wiped his mouth with a tissue and took a puff from his rescue inhaler. "I try not to use this thing too much. You know how it goes." The inhaler went back in his pocket. "Sorry. Look, my intuition of forty years in practice tells me her problem isn't physical."

"Jazzy?" Stephen shook his head. "Yeah, but she'd never malinger."

"Didn't mean that, Steve. She left a message with Stacie that she went back to work this morning. Cancelled her follow up."

"So, what's the problem?"

"I think something big and serious happened to her. I can read behind the monotone she was spitting out. Stacie mentioned it too. I'm sure Jasmine's emotionally upset, maybe a death in the family?"

"Oh." Stephen sat upright. "I hope nothing bad has happened. Paula and I love her like a sister. I'll have Paula call her right after work."

"Good, but if she doesn't answer, go there, huh?"

#   #   #

That evening Paula and Stephen kept ringing the doorbell and knocking on Jasmine's apartment door until it finally opened a crack. Bloodshot eyes peered out from the gloom inside. "Oh, you might as well come in. I've got it coming."

As they stepped in, Stephen ventured, "Someone die?"

"No, I'll bet it's a man problem," Paula corrected. She put her face close to hers. "Right, Jazzy?"

A tear appeared on Jasmine's cheek, and Paula embraced her. "I know, baby. I know."

A light went on in Stephen's head. "Derek! That rat fink. What, he's got a wife in Mexico or something?"

Paula walked her over to the couch to sit and sob together. Jasmine croaked: "Nah, he just *dumped* me. Saturday night Derek got me drunk and convinced me we were going to be married and took me to his apartment. Then two days later he breaks the news, all casual-like, that he's going away to Arizona—makes it completely obvious he never loved me."

"That jerk!" Stephen shook his head. "But that guy's not even *close* to the marrying type, Jazzy. Didn't you believe what everyone was telling you about him?"

"Course I didn't. Doesn't handsome, completely charming and rich count for anything?"

Paula tilted her head against Jasmine's. "Not without love, my dear. Not without love."

"Of course, and I know it's all my fault, guys. I'm so *embarrassed*. Everyone must be laughing at me. I think I'll apply to another hospital."

Stephen said. "Ah, it'll blow over in a week."

Paula turned to him. "That's just insensitive, dear. I don't think you understand how painful this is for her."

Jasmine straightened up and turned to him. Stephen was walking around her living room looking at the pictures on the wall. "That's all right, Steve. I've been a bad host. Um, would you like some coffee?"

"Uh, sure."

Jasmine started to get up but Paula restrained her so she called out, "Steve, it's all made. Just go in the kitchen and push the on button." She coughed. "And help yourself to those chocolate chip cookies in the little tin. I made them to surprise Der…"

Stephen emerged from the kitchen munching. "Man, these are *great*, Jazzy."

Jasmine's voice was a croaky loud whisper. "Sorry, I'm out of milk and cream."

"No problem. I like it black. Say, if Marston ever tasted these he might not have taken off."

Paula spoke with the resonant firmness of a school principal. "Steve, dear, why don't you go down to that little market we passed on the way over and get us some milk and half and half? Your coffee will be brewed when you get back."

"Look, I don't use any."

Paula squinted and leveled her gaze at him. "Don't take the car, Steve. It's just two blocks—the walk will do you some good."

"Huh? Oh, I get it." He stuffed a cookie in his breast pocket and headed for the door. "Back in little while."

#   #   #

Paula had a little purse hanging on her left side so her short arm could open the flap. When the door closed, she reached in, removed a bar of semi-sweet chocolate and offered it to Jasmine. "We need to talk, girl."

While Jasmine played with opening the wrapper, Paula grabbed a tissue box, got a straight chair and dragged it in front of her. She sat, and took her friend's hands in hers. "Look, Miss Tynan, You're one of the smartest people I know. You graduated top of your nursing class from a wheelchair, but when it comes to men you can be, uh, shall we say: a bit retarded."

"Yeah, I guess, but don't worry. I'll get over this— maybe in ten years."

"Okay, Jazzy, first, you *know* we're 'family' here. Will you promise never to keep things like this from me again?"

Silent tears had begun to flow again. She nodded. "Uh huh."

"You really were in love with Derek, right?"

"Uh huh."

"But now you *know* that there's no love in his little black heart and it's all over."

"Uh--" (hic) "Uh huh."

"Will you promise that your next man will be a man of God who truly loves you?"

Jasmine rolled her eyes to the ceiling and sighed. "Yeah."

"Will you pray for God to help you with this right now, and will you start coming to church with us again?"

Jasmine took a tissue, wiped her eyes and blew her nose. "But I'll have to face all those people."

"We'll face them together, Jazzy."

She nodded. "Okay, I will, Paula. I *will*."

"We discovered the Lord together, remember? You had just become paralyzed and were having suicidal thoughts. I want you to recall the joy we both had in abiding in Him. I still do. Even without earth friends, we're never alone, right? You know what you're your guardian angel would tell you, right?"

"Andrew? Yeah, I can imagine."

"Just ask God to abide with you again."

"I'll…" She sniffed, "try. Paula, all I ever wanted was a real family: a husband—children. Is that too much to ask?"

Paula dropped her head and tilted it as if she were trying to peer under Jasmine's drooped eyelids. "I know it's going to take awhile, Jazzy, but remember, you won't go through this all by yourself. We're here for you and we're praying for you. When you're ready, you will even forgive Derek so you can move on without scars."

"What?"

"I don't mean like ask him back or even *like* him. Just forgiveness before the Lord for those who have hurt you."

"Don't know about that one."

"I understand. It's early. Meanwhile, it will help if we can get back into a normal routine. There are some things I could use your help with."

"Really? What should I do first?"

"First? Lets do something to help you forget that certain someone. I say we eat all of those cookies before Steve gets back."

FIVE

God had created an earth-like planet in Heaven as a training ground for guardian angels. The grass along the riverbank was dark and verdant under the royal purple sky. An auburn-haired girl angel relaxed on a flat rock on a hillside above the stream, running her toes through the grass. An ocelot sat on the grass next to her, his head resting on her lap. She massaged the cat's neck and he began a loud purr.

Angela stood over the child, spread out her white wings, and crouched down to her eye level. "Look, Susie, don't you dare give up. You did just *fine* considering it was your first flight."

She looked up with a tight-lipped frown. "Did not. You saw it. I slid sideways--almost crashed into a tree."

"Oh, phish. You missed it, didn't you?" She put her hands on her hips. "Most don't do as well as you this early, but you'll tire out when you start panic-flapping. Gliding some of the time is important, and that's the easy part."

Susie pouted and shrugged her little wings.

"Relax. Go with the flow, sweetie." Angela jumped up in the air and flew slow circles around Susie with easy, graceful strokes."

"Sure, easy for you," the little voice called up to her.

Angela began to glide back in a descending spiral and landed with a grin. "See, no flapping at all as I came down, and I'm not winded. Give it a try, huh?"

Susie got up but pointed overhead to a rapidly descending angel. "Oooh, will you look at him dive!"

Just when it looked like he would crash into the lawn, the angel cupped his wings, slowed, and gently touched down. Susie stood watching, her mouth agape. Angela whispered. "That's an advanced technique, but nothing you can't do one day."

Andrew folded his wings and grinned. "Hi, Angela. How's your pupil doing?"

"Just fine, Mister Showoff. She's working on a little courage, is all."

Andrew bent over and brought his squinting face close to Susie's. "I know just the thing to get her over that. I'll carry her way up high…" He gestured with one wing. "Then I'll just *fling* her over a cloud."

Susie covered her mouth and let out a short scream. Angela stamped her foot, hands on hips. "Stop it, you. Still like scaring the girls, huh?"

Andrew gave a sideways smirk at Angela but squatted down in front of Susie. He spoke with a big grin and he softened his voice. "You know, Susie, I have it on *good* authority: a week from now you'll be gliding over that river below with your friends and laughing with joy."

"Uh, not sure…"

"Oh, *I'm* sure. 'Cause you've got the best teacher around, and always remember His Spirit is always present inside to help you too. Don't forget to ask 'cause He always listens."

Susie offered a weak smile to Angela. "Well, maybe."

Andrew's finger went up. "No maybes. Done deal. Look, I need to talk with your teacher for a while. Your friends are on the riverbank down there. Show us a few big strokes and join them." He picked up the cat, handed it to Angela, and gestured toward the river. "No walking."

Susie's brow came down, and she brought her lips together in determination. She flashed Angela a glance and took off with furious strokes. She listed a bit left, but stayed airborne. When she started gliding, they applauded.

Angela said, "Susie gets better every time." She opened her hands toward Andrew. "And why are we graced with your presence today?"

Andrew studied the pink-tinged clouds for a moment. "Oh, just thought it would be good to discuss our respective Earth charges once in a while. How's Stephen doing?"

"Ah, so good, Andrew. He and Paula have an infant and I'm such good friends with her guardian, Sheerah. But I haven't seen your charge lately. Jasmine okay?"

"She has a huge crush on one of the doctors at her hospital."

"Right. I remember Stephen talking about him. What's his name?"

"Pond Scum."

"Songbird" laughter from Angela. "Oh, oh. I get the picture, but what's his real name?"

"Derek Marston, and they just broke up. That's a good thing, of course, but Jasmine's really upset. Thought I'd ask your advice as a woman on how to encourage her."

Angela forced him to make eye contact with her wide blue eyes. "Andrew," she grinned, "What did *Jesus* tell you to say?"

"Oh, well…" Suddenly, some angels flying overhead seemed to interest him. "Well, He told me to whisper about His ever-present love, of course, and remind her of some words she'd read in the Bible. Truth is, Jasmine hasn't prayed for a while. She's done nothing but think about that man and cry like crazy."

Angela shrugged. "But you did your duty. These things just take time, huh?"

"I know, but Jasmine is *real* unhappy. She's not even going to church, and some demons have been sneaking up and whispering things too. I thought you might think of something else I could speak to her spirit. Lately, I've been wishing I could jump down out of the dimension portal, give her a big hug, and encourage her face-to-face."

Angela released a "wind chime" giggle. "Andrew, you *do* know you're starting to sound just like me, don't you?"

He threw up his hands. "I wouldn't actually do that. You know I wouldn't. It's just that we really *know* Jazzy, and she's special to both of us. We were standing on Earth right beside her when the Master healed her legs." His face went slack. "Can't you think of *anything* that might cheer her up?"

"I can." Angela nodded. "I'll encourage some humans she knows to give her those hugs she needs. There's Steve and Paula, of course, but there's also someone else I'm thinking of—and I'm guessing he'd be *perfect* for her."

Andrew's jaw dropped. He squinted at her. "Angie! You've been nosing around in the affairs of my charge again, haven't you?"

"Jazzy's *my* friend too, Andrew." Wind chime giggles.

SIX

Jasmine sat at a table in the nurse's lounge, face buried in her hands. She became aware of a large, gentle hand being placed on her shoulder and the back of her neck. She flinched. The hand withdrew for a moment but came back. She let it rest, not turning to see who it was. She knew, and the comfort she felt through that firm touch was too pleasant to disturb.

"I'm betting..." He began to knead the tense shoulder gently. Jasmine felt her muscles relax. "I'm betting it won't be long before we'll all be enjoying watching you dance through these halls again."

She forced herself to straighten up, turn, and glance up at him, but was glad the massage continued, now with both shoulders. "Sam, I'm so embarrassed. Just *everyone* knows, don't they?"

He withdrew his hands, and she regretted the loss. "Of course, Jazzy. This place is like an ongoing soap opera." He chuckled. "But you just smile in their face if anyone stares at you."

Jasmine took out a tissue and blew her nose lightly. "They all know how *stupid* I've been. Everyone was warning me, and you were right: even Mindy."

Samuel picked up the tissue she left on the table, rolled it in his palms, and hooked it into a corner wastebasket. The "ball" just missed Susan, a middle-aged Asian nurse sipping tea. She shook her head side to side. "Doctor's lounge is at the other end of the hall."

Samuel laughed. "Ahh, that's a *work* station, Susan. Your lounge is so much more fun."

Jasmine's expression turned to amusement. He took her hand, turning her toward him. She was startled by it's warmth as they made eye contact. "Jazzy, you did nothing wrong. You know, I've often felt the translators got a word wrong in Corinthians thirteen."

"Do tell."

"Yeah, it says 'love is kind.' I'll bet the original Greek was: 'love is blind.'"

Jasmine sighed. "I know. I know." She pulled her hand away. "Maybe they left out the stupid part, too, but I'll be all right, Sam. I just need some time."

"Course you will. I think you could have your pick of any single male in this hospital."

"Oh, stop it." She giggled. "Quit lying to make me feel better. Anyway, I'm taking my friend Paula's advice and avoiding all men for the time being."

"Good plan." Samuel stood up straight. "After that, try someone a bit older and more responsible." His grin showed the fine wrinkles of northern Europeans who like the sun.

Jasmine's eyes twinkled as she caught the hidden meaning. "You're not suggesting some friendly father figure like *yourself*, are you?"

Feigning a heart attack, Samuel clutched his chest. "Father figure? Aargh, that hurt."

"Oh, I'm sorry, but you are a lot older, aren't you?"

He croaked: "Seven years and two months. I just happen to know."

Jasmine got up, suppressing a grin. "Oh, here's Linda. I have to get back on the floor." She pointed at his hair. "I'll apologize, but you do have gray streaks in your temples, you know. Although I'll admit they are a nice match for your eyes."

Samuel brought his face nearer and gave his temples a stroke. "I bleach those streaks in so my patients won't know how young I am."

Susan laughed loudly and walked off.

SEVEN

Paula wrestled with a large painting in the exhibit hall. "Jazzy, could you help this one-armed woman and lift up the other end. Careful, it's heavy."

They hoisted it up to the hanger. "Paula, do you really think this will sell a lot for the Disabled Society? I mean, you're the only celebrity here."

"Ah, you just wait and see." She chuckled. "And I'm not some big shot just because I won the Art Museum contest. The public is curious to see what foot or mouth painters can do, and some will be shocked at this quality. You remember Kurt Williams. He did this one."

Jasmine stepped back to admire the work they had just put up. "No argument about that, but how much cash will they donate?"

"Our only profit won't be that donation box at the door. Some of these paintings will sell for serious change."

Jasmine picked up a portrait work and placed it on the peg next to the large one. "But don't these artists need the money for themselves?"

"Sure, and they sell them in the lobby at the Society, but not many customers come there. The works they've brought here to sell are on a fifty-fifty basis. and believe me, they're excited about funding an elevator to our new painting loft."

Jasmine turned around at the sound of a baby crying. Stephen was cradling David in his arms and swinging him around. She hurried to him. "Oh, please, can I hold him?"

As soon as the infant snuggled next to Jasmine he became quiet. She kissed the top of his head and walked to Paula. "He's just *beautiful*, you guys. Anytime you want a sitter, just call."

Paula laughed. "Careful what you say. We'll definitely take you up on that." Stephen nodded. "Oh yeah."

The infant began making fussy sounds. Jasmine scowled at Stephen. "So, you didn't notice why your boy was crying?"

He held out his hands, puzzled. "What?"

Jasmine asked Paula, "Where'd you put the diaper stash?"

Paula reached out. "Here, I'll take him."

"No, no. I'm glad to do it. I have to show you my babysitting credentials. Besides, I came here to help you out."

"As a registered nurse, you don't have to prove anything." She pointed. "But the bag's over there in that corner, and you know where the ladies' room is. Thanks."

When Jasmine left, Paula said, "I think she's doing much better these days, don't you?"

"Yeah, when she's with us she almost seems like her old self, but I've been talking with Sam Wright. He says she's still struggling."

"It's just gonna take time. She's so, *so* sensitive to what people think of her, and I'm worried she hasn't been to church like she promised. We all need divine help with life's speed bumps, right?"

Paula pointed to a side wall. "Could you grab those folding chairs and set them up in a row right here. There's a dear."

Stephen returned dragging a half-dozen chairs. "Remember I told you I saw my guardian Angela on the church rafter two Sundays ago with another angel woman? The other one was swinging her legs and happy, but I could tell Angie was searching for someone. I'll bet it was Jasmine."

"You're right, Steve. I'll try a little more gentle persuasion. If I can convince her to come along with us next time, maybe she'll agree to talk with pastor Jim."

A middle-aged man with a crew cut and a ruddy, perspiration-covered face huffed up in a wheelchair. "Hey, Paula, sorry I'm late. Is there still room?"

She skipped over to him, gave him a shoulder squeeze and a mock sad face. "Oh, I'm so sorry, Colonel, all the spots are taken. Try again next year."

He returned her laugh with a grin. "I know you're kidding. This guy a friend of yours?"

She gestured. "My husband, Steve. Steve, this is Mike Duggan. He's a real war hero and a watercolor artist extraordinaire."

Mike leaned to one side, looked around Stephen and spoke to the approaching figure. "And I know this gal with the sexy legs. Hi Jazzy. You never told us about having a baby."

"Hi, Mike." Jasmine stood next to Paula, gazed into the infant's face and swung him gently side to side. "He's Paula's, but I think I'll keep him."

Mike nodded and turned to Paula. "Well, *that* explains why you haven't been around so much. Seriously: congratulations. What's the baby's name?"

"He's our David, and, yes, he certainly keeps us busy."

"Say, Paula, I've got a crate with six paintings on the loading dock. You got anyone to move them in?"

"Why yes." She gestured to her husband. "We have Stephen Schwartz here. His M.D. stands for Moving Director and he's an expert."

Stephen flashed a pout at his wife, turned and headed off. "Sure, Mike. I'll bring them right up."

Mike swiveled his chair around and hollered. "Hey, MD." When Stephen turned around, he pointed to a furniture dolly. "Mister Expert, you might want to take that along with you."

EIGHT

Stephen carried the rest of the dinner dishes into the kitchen where Paula was rinsing plates for the dishwasher. "After all that was said, I was surprised Jasmine didn't show up at church yesterday. I know you talked with her about it. You know, the time you wanted to talk in private."

"I did. Pass the silverware." She rinsed them and began to drop each one into the washer cups. "I did think it was all settled and I expected her. I even called her again on Saturday to confirm, but she didn't answer."

The kitchen phone rang and Stephen checked the ID. "I have to take this. It's a doctor at the hospital." He picked it up with one hand and passed Paula an empty wine glass with the other.

"Hi, Sam. What can I do for you?"

A monotone voice full of gravel responded. "Steve, I have something important to show you and Paula. May I stop in for a moment on my way home."

"Of course, Sam. What is it?"

"I have to show you this in person, all right? I'll be there in ten."

Paula closed the washer door and turned it on. "He's coming over? Our   living room looks like a teen lounge."

"I'll help straighten up." He chuckled. "That was Sam Wright. Wants to talk with both of us. Don't worry. Look, he's probably just dropping off some annoying, new politically correct regulation from the hospital. He's on the board, you know."

"But if he wants to see me too, maybe it's about Jazzy. He's always liked her you know. Sam used to take two or three wheelchair people to events regularly, and Jazzy was always one of them. He'd rent a large van and they'd go off to things like the County Fair, the Scottish Trials or sometimes that big lake with the beach."

"Funny, he never mentioned that to me."

#   #   #

Samuel arrived with a deeply worried expression creasing his face. "Can we talk frankly about Jasmine? I'm guessing you must know what's going on with her."

Paula escorted him to the living room. "Jasmine? I'm afraid we don't know anything new, Sam. Haven't heard from her for a few days. You want to have some dessert?

Samuel turned to Stephen and bit his lip. Stephen grasped his arm. "Sam, something happen to her?"

"I…" Sam appeared to summon up courage. "Did you hear she quit her job this weekend?"

Paula jerked back. "What? Jazzy *loves* her nursing job."

Stephen said, "You're *sure*?"

"Jazzy came to the hospital yesterday. It was a Sunday and I wasn't working. She cleaned out her locker and left a formal letter of immediate resignation on the Administrator's desk.

"My God," Paula clutched her cheeks. "No reason? Nothing?"

"None. Well, her letter said "immediate personal concerns." I thought she must have talked with you. You're her best friend."

"Not a *word*, Sam. She's been overly sensitive. She still imagines people are talking about her breakup with Derek, but she's been calmer lately. Maybe there was some serious confrontation with someone at the hospital?"

"None that I know of, Paula." He pulled out a piece of paper from his pocket. "She left this in my mail slot. Looks like an afterthought."

Jasmine's note was written on a piece of scrap paper: *Sam, I want you to know my leaving has nothing to do with you. Sorry, I had to break our first date on Saturday, if that's what it was. You are a wonderful man and a good friend. Please ask Paula Schwartz to come to my apartment. Jasmine.*

Paula let out a squeak and punched in a number on her cell phone. "If she wants me to visit her, maybe we're okay. I'll bet she's decided to look for a job with a small group practice somewhere—a job where no one knows her story. She's been a silly girl before. I ought to know."

She pocketed the phone in her purse. "Still not answering, and the voice mail's full. I think I'll just go over there right now and settle this thing."

Sam was busy pacing and scratching his head. "I hope you won't mind if I come with you?"

NINE

Half a dozen people were in the apartment lobby chatting when the three arrived. Paula went to Jasmine's mailbox and awkwardly shifted her baby to her short arm so she could go through her purse. "Uh oh, she's removed her name from the box."

Stephen squinted in. "But there's some mail. You find the key. Here, I'll take David."

Paula rummaged a bit, came up with the right key, and pulled out two bills from the box. "I'll take these up to her. Let's go. I have her apartment key if we need it."

There being no answer to the bell and knocking, Paula opened the door. They gasped at the sight of empty rooms. Samuel stood immobile by the door, chewing on a knuckle. The others walked around the vacant apartment.

Paula found an envelope on the kitchen counter sitting on top of Jasmine's cell phone. Inside, she had placed two hundred dollars in cash, credit cards cut in half, and a note that read: *Paula, this should cover any bills not on autopay. I am leaving here, but please know that I love you both. Do not waste your time trying to find me. Goodbye, J.*

They faced each other in bewilderment. Oh my God," Stephen exclaimed. "She's really *gone!*"

"But this makes no sense, Steve. She was doing so well just days ago,"

"I don't know how you feel, but I'm *not* about to do what she's asking. I say we try to find her."

"Darn right. I..." The baby began to fuss and Paula took him back. "I don't care what it takes, Steve. Something *bad* has happened. I know it."

The sound of loud sobbing behind them caused them to swivel around. Sam, still standing by the door, was weeping into his hands.

Stephen and Paula hurried to him, and Stephen put his arm around his shoulders. "Hey, man, I'm sure she's okay. It'll be all right."

"Oh no, it won't. Not even close."

Paula's voice melted into softness. "I'm guessing Jasmine means more to you than we thought, huh?"

Samuel nodded. "Yup." He took the tissue Stephen pulled out of his pocket, blew his nose, and croaked: "Saturday was gonna be our first date, but I've been trying to get her to notice me long before she was healed and out of that chair."

Stephen gave him a shoulder squeeze. "Cheer up, man. We'll find this crazy girlfriend of yours even if we have to hire a private detective."

Samuel's eyes flared as he turned intently to Stephen. "We will, and I'm paying for it."

TEN

In its historical past, the office building in downtown Denver had once been clean and modern, but with a deteriorating community now surrounding it, the building now served a clientele less concerned with appearance. Paula, Stephen and Samuel were in an elevator heading to the fifth floor. Paula said, "You never told me how much this guy is costing us."

Samuel pouted a bit. "Let's just say he costs more per hour than your babysitter. Did everyone follow up on the assignments he asked for?"

The door slid open. Paula sighed. "Sure, but a lot of good it will do us."

The receptionist motioned them into the office, where they would sit and await the entrance of their Missing Persons Detective, Roger Flynn. Before them was an enormous black, carved Chinese antique desk strewn with papers. Flynn had framed newspaper articles touting court cases on the walls, and a bookcase full of law books that appeared untouched. Sam would later mention that the computer on his desk was at least ten years old.

Flynn ambled in a side door, leaned back on the front of his desk to face them, and rested his foot on a carved dragon that seemed to growl from the desk corner. His tweed sport jacket covered a discordant Hawaiian shirt, and his face reminded Paula of Henry Kissinger.

They had stood up when he came in, but he grinned and motioned them to sit down. "So, tell me more about our disappearing lady. Each of you asked all your mutual acquaintances about recent events, I trust." He pointed at Paula. "And you are?"

"Paula, her good friend. Sure, I spoke to everyone she knows at the disabled center and our church. Pretty much, they all said the same thing: that she seemed to be coming out of her depression from the breakup. A week before this, several of us laid hands on her and prayed for a new beginning in her life. Of course, talking about Derek directly made her uncomfortable, so maybe that's why she's avoided friends by skipping church."

"I get it. No talk of travel anywhere or trouble at the hospital?"

"No, nothing like that."

"You men are both doctors, huh?" He nodded to Stephen. "Anything medical going on with our subject?"

"By 'subject,' you mean our beloved Jasmine. No, no known medical problems, Roger. Her doctor is my partner,

John Anderson. He said she had a severe grief reaction, but came out of it with the usual ups and downs. A routine blood test showed no sign of infection or anemia. She's a healthy woman."

"So we can likely rule out a terminal illness she wants to keep secret." Roger flashed the "finger gun" at Samuel. He flinched and jumped up, then began circling the room.

"Mind if I walk while I talk?"

Paula gave Roger a pained smile. "Poor Sam. He kinda likes Jazzy."

Samuel paced for a moment, indulging their patience. "All right, I did speak to everyone who knew Jasmine at our hospital, both friends and coworkers. Most said the same thing the others did. I really don't know why she thought they'd keep making fun of her. She was so *darned* sensitive, so caring, so…"

He stopped and leaned on the door frame. "Even her women friends loved her just like I…" That ended with a croak. He took out a tissue and blew his nose. "Sorry."

Stephen said, "Hey, man, take your time. We understand, but quit with the past tense."

Samuel stood up straight and blew out through his cheeks. "I guess you should know; it wasn't all rosy. The truth is, some women are genuinely jealous of her, and they've made some nasty comments. I heard one myself. It was right behind her back, so she couldn't miss it."

"How'd she react in general?"

"Her real friends said she had some crying spells, but that was only right after the breakup. Lately, she seems to have ignored what little snickering was still around."

Stephen raised a finger. "And that's all normal psychology."

Roger gestured in agreement. "Sounds about right, Sam. So no reports of any big blow up with anyone, you know, cat fights?"

"Not at all. Her friends would know if something like that happened, but I should mention what one of those friends told me about her on the Sunday she came to resign and pack up. She said Jasmine was all pale and twitchy--looked terrified."

"Roger nodded. "*That* could be significant. Remember, hurtful things can happen behind the scenes, and you never really know what a subject is thinking. She could be reacting to e-mails, phone calls, even a meeting on the street, but for now we'll leave those ideas open."

He leaned forward and gestured for Samuel to sit. "Missing persons are easier to find when the subject just moves somewhere, even if they change their name. The hardest cases are finding people who are determined *not* to be found. Did you know she cancelled her Email server?"

Shaky heads all around. "But so far, here's what I found…" He went behind his desk and stood, leaning forward on his hands. "Her bank accounts are still intact. Please don't ask me how I know some things."

Paula brightened. "So you can tell where she is from those?"

"If only she'd write some checks or use a credit card, but she left them behind, as you know. What Jasmine *did* do is cash out her savings, a bit over two thousand, but her checking account has a direct deposit still due in from the hospital. If she takes out more cash, I'll know where she did it."

Stephen smiled. "That's cool. Let us know when that happens. Say, what about her moving company?"

"No such thing. She gave it all to The Salvation Army. See, she's being really clever."

"Shoot. Well, how about reporting her license plate to the police?"

"They don't consider her a missing person yet. Hard to believe, but true. However, if she gets a ticket or is in an accident, I'll know where that was, and the moment I find anything, I'll call you."

Samuel's voice was still hoarse. "But in the meantime, what else will you be doing to find Jazzy?"

"Being patient and vigilant. We need a break to figure out where she might be headed. Parents are out of the picture, I assume?"

Paula said, "Father's deceased. Mother lives in New York, I think, but they haven't been in touch. She does have a sister named Mary Stearns, but they don't talk much, and I can't remember where she lives, wait—uh, West Coast, I'm pretty sure."

Roger stood up. "I'll follow up on that. All right, everyone. My advice right now is not to be discouraged. As I mentioned on the phone, results are not guaranteed, but we typically find these individuals through our network. For now, your assignment is to keep talking to Jasmine's friends. Ask about little details they thought were unimportant."

He spread out his hands and turned toward Samuel. "I do have several things I'm working on, but if there are no other questions today, come back here at the same time in one week." As they turned to leave, he spoke to their backs. "Oh, and my secretary will have your weekly statement. We take all credit cards."

#   #   #

Paula and Stephen invited Samuel to their place to get better acquainted over take-out burrito wraps. The babysitter reported that David was asleep upstairs, so they had some welcome quiet. Stephen handed Samuel one of the wraps. "Sam, you knew Jazzy before I came to Denver. I know Paula went to school with her, but how did you meet her?"

Samuel looked into the distance, and a smile formed on his face. "I was pretty new with the Mountain Medical Group then. We had some disabled patients, and I would sometimes do their checkups at the Activity Center. I saw her on the first day—a mop of red hair zipping around in her chair, grabbing arms and making people laugh."

Paula chuckled. "And she's no different now. Always high energy, and she never wanted a motorized chair. You ever notice her biceps, guys?"

Stephen put tongue in cheek. "I'm told you swing a pretty mean fry pan yourself, Paula."

Samuel sighed, gaze still focused in the distance. "So, I got on my knees in front of her chair once and asked about how I could help a patient of mine I'd seen talking with her. Before she answered, she had a giggle fit, took my hands, put them together, and said: 'As long as you're on your knees, doctor, you should either pray or propose." He laughed. "Jazzy turned my heart to mush right there."

"But Sam," Paula said. "Did you know that only a year before that, Jasmine was in a nursing home on suicide watch?

That's when we found the Lord together, and I insisted she move in with me."

"I never believed that suicide rumor."

"Oh, it was real. Her first reaction was that she'd rather die than live a life with half a body. Those are her words, and she was building up a stash of drugs. Her plan was to take them all at once when she had had enough."

Samuel searched Paula's face. "Paula, thank you so much for saving her."

"Hey, she saved me once too, and anyway, God gets the credit for both of us."

Stephen clapped his hands together lightly. "But on to practical matters. If Flynn finds her in some city, do we leave it to him, or go there ourselves?"

Samuel shook his head. "Course we'd all want to go, but we have to be sure she's staying put first or we'd just lose her."

"And if she saw us first, it could frighten her into deeper hiding."

"Right, Steve," Paula said. "Flynn might be a little weird, but he's the expert in this, not us."

Stephen tossed a hand in the air. "All right. I don't like it, but we'll see what he does with that network of his first."

Samuel rolled up the burrito wrapper and leveled a furrowed brow at Stephen. "Okay, but since we're confiding in each other, do you mind if I ask you a personal question?"

"Course not, Shoot."

"I know this can't be true, but there's a persistent rumor that you got fired from Genomics for making up a genome and claiming it was from an angel. Where'd that crazy idea come from?"

Paula started laughing, and Stephen rolled his eyes at the ceiling. Samuel tossed his hands up. "I know, I know it's crazy, but I just had to ask."

Stephen leaned toward him, a twinkle in his eye. "First, tell me this. Do you believe angels are real, Sam?"

"Of course. They're in the Bible, and I go to a Pentecostal church."

"Ever seen one yourself?

"No, but I know two people from my church who say they have."

"Think they're crazy?"

"Course not. That's discernment of spirits. I'm guessing you're about to tell me you've seen one too, huh."

"She dropped down on my car seat a couple of years ago to save my life. Her name's Angela. She lived as a human with Paula and Jazzy for a while, but that's another story. Later, she introduced Paula to her guardian-- kind of a shy girl angel named Sheerah. Your girlfriend's guardian is Andrew. He's a cool guy, and I sure hope he's on the job right now."

Samuel stared at them, slack-jawed. He spoke just above a whisper. "You don't sound like you're making this up."

Paula tapped his hand. "We're not making this up, Sam."

Samuel chuckled and shook his head. "Wow. Really?"

With a finger point, Stephen added: "And Angela's DNA pattern is on my home computer. I'll show it to you later if you like. It's being studied by my old professor at Duke, and its information should lead to treatments for genetic diseases."

"Wow." Samuel laughed. "And wow again. For *real,* huh?"

"Oh yeah, but *please* don't tell anyone," Paula begged. "We'd prefer not to have the tabloids knocking at our door."

"But, Sam, when we talk with Jazzy, and we *will* be talking with her, you can ask about Andrew. He was praying with us when she was healed."

ELEVEN

"Doctor Schwartz, there's a Doctor McPherson for you on line two. Sorry to bother you."

Stephen sat in his office. He replied with his mouth full of turkey sandwich. "I'll take it. Thanks, Stacie." He gave a few more vigorous chews and a gulp. "Hi, Angus. We were just talking about you the other day. What's up?"

"I'm guessing you're on lunch break, Mountain Time. Okay to talk now?"

"Perfect timing, Professor, if you don't mind my munching. Paula used Panini bread for my sandwich. It's delicious but a bit of a jaw workout."

"Steve, we are about to launch our first major publication on the angel DNA you gave us. Last chance to have your name on it."

"No thanks. I'd rather avoid publicity. I saw your paper on Tay Sachs disease, though. Does capping the bad gene sequence with an epigene really cure it?"

"It really does, and there are a lot more applications to come. We are collaborating with three other centers so hopefully we won't be badly ridiculed when we muster the courage to claim we have an angelic gene sequence."

"Some will zing you anyway." He chuckled. "But they'll eat crow later. We have two videos of her singing in that cathedral."

"Every time I look at this gene sequence, I'm in awe, Steve. It's such a perfect creation, it's brought me to my knees more than once. Don't laugh, but I've been going to church and I accepted Christ as my Savior."

"I'm not laughing, I'm congratulating. I'll leave the laughter to your university colleagues. Man, and especially intellectual men, don't like to admit there's a God who is smarter than they are, much less in charge of the universe." Chuckle. "It's an inconvenient truth."

"Oh, Steve, before I forget. Do I have permission to use your cell phone picture of Angela in our article?"

"No problem, Angus, but crop the rest of us out, okay?"

"Sure, and we plan to announce this as a new species when we go to press."

"Still in the genus 'homo,' though. Right? Say, in that case, you get to give it a name, don't you?"

"We've done that, but if *you* were the one choosing it, what would you pick?"

"Humph. I don't know. Maybe 'Homo Angelesis.'"

"We spent months on this, Steve, and I've talked with our collaborators too, but it was my new pastor who hit it on the head."

"And...?"

"We're going to call Angela's species 'Homo Gloria.'"

TWELVE

Stephen came home from the office on Thursday night and was greeted at his door by a friend of Paula's from work, who was holding David in her arms. "Hi, Gwen. Is Paula okay?"

"Oh, she's fine, but you're going out tonight on short notice, and I'm babysitting. She's upstairs getting dressed."

Steve winced. "Uh oh. I hope I didn't forget an occasion."

Gwen waved him upstairs. "Nah, you're safe. Go."

Paula was combing her hair in the mirror when Stephen came up behind her with a welcome kiss on her neck. She squeaked, turned, and returned the favor. "Mister Flynn called a half hour ago. He wants us to come to his office at seven thirty. Says he has some new ideas about Jasmine. Doctor Sam will be there too."

"But that's two hours from now. Did you have time to make anything for dinner?"

"I did. I made reservations."

Stephen laughed. "Clever girl."

#   #   #

Their private detective met them at his office door with a grin. "Hello everyone. It's just the four of us, so we'll sit in the waiting area where the chairs are more comfortable." He gestured behind him toward the reception desk. "There's some leftover cake from Gina's birthday, and she made fresh coffee before she left. Help yourself."

Roger pulled over a straight chair for himself, turned it around, and sat with his arms over the back. "While you are getting comfortable, let me say that I still don't know where Jasmine is, but I do have a promising theory on why she left."

Stephen dropped into a sofa chair. "Good, because if you're hoping for something new from us, we got zip."

"My approach to these cases is this. First, I learn as much as I can about the background of my subject. Jasmine is interesting to say the least. Paula, you've known her since eighth grade, and you were there when she supposedly lost the use of her legs. I'd say you are her closest friend since you shared an apartment with her for over ten years."

"What do you mean 'supposedly' lost her legs?"

"Well, I was amazed to find that you two were in the papers last year, capturing a jewel thief at your place. She helped you from her wheelchair?"

Paula laughed. "It was more like a wild, losing struggle for two minutes before the police saved us. I hit him on the head with a pan, but he started to wake up. Jazzy pushed out of her chair, fell on the man, and helped tie him up. I'm sure the angels were helping us, too."

"The angels?" He looked at the ceiling, suppressing his heaving laughter. "And yet, shortly after that, it seems your friend was up, dancing around, and looking for men and a new job. Enlighten me, please."

"Several of us prayed for her, and God healed her completely. I was there."

Roger stared at Paula with lowered eyebrows. "You're just going to leave me with that? You do know most of these cases turn out to be people faking their injury for insurance and sympathy."

"I shared an apartment with her for a long time. Believe me, she was a paraplegic."

"Legs without working nerves end up atrophied, Paula. I saw a picture of Jasmine at your wedding, and her legs would have looked good walking down the red carpet."

"Before that, they looked like long white string beans, and insensitive to pain."

"Paula, be straight with me. We're in confidence here. I won't blab to the disability insurer. You *know* that can't happen."

"Our Lord is the God of all flesh. Nothing is too hard for Him."

Stephen piped in. "I was there, too, Roger. I saw it happen."

Samuel added, "I wasn't there, but I knew her before. Jasmine worked from her wheelchair, and she was a genuine paraplegic."

"So I guess you're all telling me I'm wrong about the 'no God' idea."

All three said: "Yes."

Roger blew out through his cheeks. "All right, then. I'll let that go, but let me tell you what I found out about this boyfriend of hers. Derek Marston seems to have a spotless record, at least as far as the police are concerned. However, his father, Donald Marston, definitely does not. Donald is a very wealthy man, owner of two corporations and acquitted three times of fraud, money laundering, and insider trading."

Paula said, "Wow, what about his mother?"

"Derek's real mother, whoever she is, dropped him on Donald's doorstep with a note that read, 'He's yours. You keep him.' Donald has had five wives and counting. Each one was in their mid twenties when he married them."

"So there was never a real mother at home. That explains a lot."

Stephen asked, "But what does that have to do with Jasmine?"

Roger finger-pointed at Paula. "That man you and Jasmine helped capture—Smirkin. Do you remember what he was accused of stealing?"

"Uncut diamonds."

"Exactly, and most were never found. At the trial, Smirkin said he 'must have dropped them when he ran' and that got the whole jury laughing. And someone helped this crook hide out in town for a long while. Can you guess what business Mister DM Senior is invested in? I'll give you a hint. It has the same 'dm' initials."

Stephen said, "Diamond market?"

"Right, and he got a whopping amount from his insurance company for the theft."

"Still no Jasmine connection."

"Patience. My theory is that Donald wanted his son to marry and carry the missing diamonds with him on his honeymoon, likely to an offshore country." He searched the faces looking at him. "But he changed his plans to spare his son the risk."

"You think he asked Jazzy to carry the loot herself?"

"Quite possibly. It's just a theory right now, but here's what I found. The day before she resigned, Jasmine not only closed her savings account but her safe deposit box as well. They were within fifteen minutes of each other, and at the same bank when Derek accessed his own safe box and closed it as well."

Paula gestured "nonsense." "There's no way Jazzy would *ever* get involved with something like this."

"Paula, she may have found that they had already involved her without her knowing about it. Quite likely, they threatened her and made her transport a package of stolen diamonds. Remember how frightened they said she was on Sunday?"

Samuel cleared his throat. "Ahem, and how do you know everything that happened at the bank?"

"You guys pay me to come up with information. You pay me well and I thank you, but no one pays me to say how I get it."

Paula said, "This is all just circumstantial."

"Right, and I did say it's just a theory for now, but I want all of you to know that *should* I find clear evidence of a crime, I have to tell the police." He let out a deep breath. "There's more evidence. Yesterday, Jasmine sold her car for cash in Las Vegas."

"Oh, goodie. That's a *great* clue. Should we all go there?"

"I have men there looking for her, but probably she has a different car and a new identity. You can get both in Vegas for cash, no problem. Also, that's a likely drop-off place for stolen goods."

"But wait." Paula bounced in her chair. "I remember now. Her sister, Mary, lives in Las Vegas. She used to write her. I'll bet she's at her house right now."

"Unfortunately, that would be the 'big house,' as they say. Mary Stearns was in Federal Prison there, but she was transferred to the penitentiary in San Diego two months ago."

"Darn." Paula shook her head. "But I still can't believe she's involved in any crime, Roger."

"We're even, Paula. I don't believe God healed her. But I saved the best evidence for last."

Stephen's hand went up. "She flew to Monte Carlo?"

Roger spoke in a low monotone. "Remember the cell phone Jasmine left behind? Of course, the memory chip was removed, but guess what? I found it bent in half on the kitchen floor, and fortunately, it's not encrypted."

He waited with a grin for that to sink in. "My man couldn't retrieve most of the data, but he got the last text and reply. On the Sunday she left, she texted Derek Marston: 'Confirmed. I have the package you gave me.' His reply was: 'Do not deliver as planned. Sending ten Bs + instructions.' The Bs refer to 'big ones,' that's ten thousand dollars, folks."

THIRTEEN

Samuel, Paula, and Stephen gathered on the sidewalk outside Flynn's office building, discussing the latest revelations. Paula took hold of Stephen's arm and looked up at him. "Steve, I'm confused now more than ever. I can't believe Jazzy's involved with criminals, but Flynn makes a good case, doesn't he?"

"Maybe we should go to Las Vegas and nose around ourselves."

Samuel said, "Or go to San Diego and talk to her sister, but I'm sure Flynn's already doing that."

Stephen raised a finger. "But here's a hole in Flynn's story. If Jazzy *did* deliver stolen goods in Vegas, why wouldn't she just come back here afterward?"

Samuel said, "Maybe those instructions were to stay out of sight, you know, lay low or else."

"Yeah. I hate to admit it, but I think we're stuck. The only thing I'm *sure* of is that Jazzy is out there somewhere and in a world of danger."

"Well, I know what we should do," Paula declared. "Let's all three of us find a quiet place and pray for her."

Samuel put his hands on their shoulders. "My condo. It's just two blocks from here, and there's a roof garden on top."

#   #   #

The three found some peace alone on Samuel's roof, surrounded by planters, benches, and potted trees. The late spring night was cool and cloudless. A half-moon, Jupiter, and a thousand stars bid them welcome.

Paula took her husband's hand with her one good arm, raised it up, and indicated he should do the same with Samuel. "Dear Heavenly Father, we three are here in your presence to ask for mercy for our beloved sister, Jasmine Tynan. On this Earth, only you know what has happened to her. Send your angel, we pray, to watch over her…"

"That would be Andrew, right?"

Paula giggled. "Yes, send that cute, curly-headed angel of hers right now and ask him to guard her from all evil, we pray."

Samuel was getting choked up again. "Yes, and *please* dear God, give her the peace and comfort she needs. Hold her in your loving arms just as I long to do right now. *Please* preserve her health and especially her *life* and…" Crying made him stop.

Stephen patted Samuel's arm while Paula continued. "And, dearest Lord, we know that you are present when two or more are gathered in your name. Hear our prayers. We *know* they are in accordance with your will, and we pray in Jesus' name. Amen."

FOURTEEN

Roger Flynn greeted Stephen at his office door that Saturday. "Hello Steve. Thanks for coming by yourself. Did you bring the sample I asked for?"

"Yes, and better than the hairs you suggested, I have a vial of Jasmine's blood. We always save some in case the lab loses theirs. But, tell me, how's her DNA going to help us?"

He gestured for him to sit, "For the same reason I wanted you to come by yourself. Her best friend and her lover would be overly upset at the mere suggestion that Jasmine might be dead."

Stephen's head jerked up. "Oh, my God! What did you find out?"

"Take it easy. Nothing definite."

"Look, I'm upset, too, but Sam's hardly her lover. He's just in *love* with her. Seriously, you don't think it's likely she's dead, do you?"

"Hopefully not, but Steve, I've been doing missing persons for a long time, and we have to consider all possibilities. In criminal cases, it's not unusual for a novice 'mule' to disappear. Less risk to the criminals if their mule gets caught and squeals."

"Novice 'mule?' This is *so* getting out of hand."

"Just being complete. I'm monitoring unidentified bodies found in Nevada and California. The police really appreciate getting DNA samples in missing person cases. Do you think suicide is a possibility for this woman?"

Stephen frowned. "Ooh, I don't know."

"Don't know? What haven't you told me?"

"As a teenager, she attempted it when she became paralyzed, but this is entirely different."

"But that's a reaction pattern. You're a doctor. You should know. Depressed again, then bam. Obviously, her trail disappears if she packs it in."

Stephen glanced at the ceiling and sighed. "Any less *macabre* ideas?"

"Sure. Some fall into drug use and join the homeless. I know how to look for newbies in these communities."

"What a relief. Hey! Have you forgotten we're talking about Jasmine here? She's about the most straight arrow person I know."

"Sorry to upset you, but I have to keep emotions out of what I do. Look, I do have something hopeful for you. Two days ago, Jasmine cashed out her checking account in Las Vegas at a small rural branch. Their camera photo confirms her identity, but her hair's been dyed brown. Anyway, we do know she was alive then."

"Great, she's fine. Why were you scaring me? Now, how about we go to Vegas and pick her up?"

"Not that easy. I had three men in the general vicinity, and one got to the bank less than an hour later. A traffic cam caught her leaving on a city bus, but my men are looking for her."

"Maybe she went to San Diego to see her sister?"

"That would be foolish of her if she wants to stay in hiding. Ms Stearns never had any visitors, but Jasmine could have called or written her, of course."

"So, visit the sister and ask."

"Stearns is due for release in less than two months. She wouldn't tell us if the two of them are planning something, and asking would only tip our hand, but we'll have her followed when she gets out."

Stephen threw up his hands. "So now you think her sister is involved and they're planning something? You're talking about unclaimed bodies and drug use, but aren't you just making up unlikely theories?"

"You pay me to be thorough."

"Yeah, well, I still say we're overlooking something."

"Plan on checking back with me in a couple of weeks. I'll call sooner if something significant turns up. Gina will give you an appointment on your way out."

#   #   #

"Dear Mary:

I brought your car down from Vegas, and it's parked in Wally's Garage lot. It's right by the exit for the penitentiary on I-8. Strange kind of car, but I guess it's perfect for my spunky little sister. A man called Jim runs the garage. I paid for the month, and asked him to charge the battery just before you are released. I taped two hundred dollars for you behind the glove box, along with the picture I had saved of us when we were kids.

I missed the weekend, or I would have visited you. I hope you find God. I seem to have lost Him along the way. Sorry, I won't be there when you get out. I'll be gone then.

Just know that I love you, Sis.

J"

#   #   #

TEXT MESSAGE for Doctor Stephen Schwartz: "Cancelling our follow-up meeting for this Saturday. I'll follow any leads if they turn up. Will contact you as needed. For now, Jasmine's trail has gone dark. Flynn"

FIFTEEN

Andrew swooped down from a higher cloud deck to join a flock of lower-flying angels. "Is Angela with your group, ladies? I must find her."

One pointed. "Pretty sure she's with that flock of ultra sopranos over there."

Powerful, rapid strokes like a frightened duck propelled Andrew ahead until he reached her. Out of breath, he grunted, "Angie—need your help--right now—emergency."

Without a word, she banked out of formation and followed Andrew in a steep glide to the top of a hill below. He landed but kept his wings extended for cooling. Angela scowled at him. "This better be important, Andy. We were all going to a rehearsal."

Andrew was still panting from his effort. "It's Jasmine. She's about to—about to take her own life."

Angela slapped a hand over her mouth, covering a shriek. "Impossible! She'd *never* do such a thing."

"Oh, I wish that were true. She hasn't been praying, and three whispering demons are following her. They're saying things like she's 'worthless now' and 'God hates her'. I got in some words myself, but it's not been enough."

"Not praying? I thought Jazzy loved Jesus. But if that's so, how did you get to speak to her at all?"

"Steve, Paula, and another man prayed for her. That gave me a Holy Spirit moment. I came in sword swinging and got close for a few moments. I tried to tell her Jesus still loves her, but I'm afraid she thinks she's a worthless sinner right now, and I can't get through. I'm asking you if you know any of God's special words I could whisper to wake her spirit. Soon it's gonna be too late."

Angela shook her head, tears beginning to stream down. "Your words alone won't help without the power of prayer, without her heart opening to them. We have to go there, both of us, and I mean in *person*."

"Angie, you *know* we can't do that. It's against all the rules, and you should know that better than anyone."

Angela fell to her knees and pointed for him to do the same. "God makes the rules, Andrew." She raised her hands upward. "Praise you, Lord, Yeshua. Praise your Holy name. We know it is not Your will for dearest Jasmine to suffer, sin, and die. We *know* how you love her, and we saw how you healed her legs. Please, we pray in your name, Yeshua. Allow us to at least *try* to save this person who is so precious to us as well."

Andrew groaned, threw up his hands, and cried out. "Oh yes, Lord. I know Your rules for us, but we have both walked in earthly dimensions with Jasmine before. Please. If You will let us serve You there again, please grant us our..."

The sudden light blinded the imploring angels. They covered their eyes with their wings and bowed their heads. As the brightness faded, each felt a gentle hand on top of their heads. His voice was firm and steady. "Please stand, good and faithful servants."

Andrew was slack-jawed and speechless, but Angela had no trouble. "Oh, thank you for listening, Yeshua, my Lord. You know we have lived on the Earth with this woman, and she is like family to us. If there is any hope we can save our beloved Jasmine, may we please be allowed to go to her and try?"

Jesus stood beside them. He smiled. "Children of God, I always listen, and I have heard many impassioned prayers for Jasmine from Earth as well. With a love as strong as theirs, and both of you share, you should know there is *always* hope and mercy."

"Oh, thank you, my Lord." Andrew bowed his head and spread his enormous wings out on the ground. "I am desperate not to fail my charge."

"Do you each of you understand that if your request is granted, you will be *as humans*, and have no special powers either here or on Earth? Jasmine is presently under the spell of the Great deceiver. Her true heart is bound up, but unless *she herself* calls to me of her free will, I will not intervene."

"Oh, yes, my Lord." Angela began to tremble. "We *know*, but is it not better to fail than to have never tried?"

Jesus replaced His hands on their heads and smiled. "You have my blessing. Your destination is 2B. Go."

SIXTEEN

Andrew stumbled forward on the sidewalk before bracing himself on a building. "Whoa, I can hardly stand here."

Angela said, "Just lean back and relax when you walk. You're not balancing the weight of your wings anymore. We're like humans now. Took me a while to get it right the first time, too."

"We don't *have* any time. No relaxing, Yeshua said 'go to be…' what? Saviors?"

"No, He put us in front of a small hotel." She headed for the door, Andrew following in a clumsy, bent-over lope. "She must be in room 2B."

Angela put her arm around his waist to help him walk more normally as they entered the lobby. She hoped her smile didn't look fake as she nodded at the registration clerk. He just gave them a puzzled glance as they headed for the stairwell. Andrew slipped and fell on one knee as they started up. "Come on, Andy. Remember, straighten up and lean *back*."

When they got to the corridor, they could hear the wailing down the hall. Andrew loped quickly toward the sound and gave a "woodpecker-like" rapping on the door to room 2B. "Are you all right?" He shouted, "Open up, please."

"I'm fine. Go away!" A woman's voice shouted from within.

He glanced at Angela. "Still alive."

Angela found the door unlocked, pushed in, and they bolted toward the moans. Jasmine sat wearing undergarments in a dry bathtub with streaks of blood on her arms, her face contorted in terror. She looked up and screamed, "Get out of here. Go away!"

She grabbed a box cutter next to her and swung it down at her bleeding wrist while Andrew was lunging toward her. He fell and slid, crashing against the tub wall, but he seized her down-swinging arm. She screamed again, "No, no. Stop. I have to die."

Andrew lay sideways on the tile floor, but held a firm grip on her arm. Angela knelt down and pried the knife away from the protesting fingers. Jasmine lashed out with her bloody free hand and struck Andrew's face while still screaming for them to go away.

He groaned with the blow but both hung onto Angela as they began to pray. "Dear Lord, cast these demons away from her, in Jesus' name."

Jasmine's eyes did not see past the veil of tears. "Who are you? Get out of here!"

When the angels released Jasmine, she collapsed in a trembling, sobbing lump on the far wall of the tub.

Angela sheathed the box cutter and slid it in her pocket, noticing for the first time that the Lord had dressed her in jeans. "You don't recognize us?"

Jasmine was gasping and panting. She wiped tears from her rheumy eyes, producing blood streaks on her cheeks. She looked from one to the other as her breathing slowed. "Angela? Andrew? You're not supposed to leave Heaven."

Angela pulled off some toilet paper and applied it to her bleeding wrist. "Yeah, well, you're not supposed to commit suicide."

Jasmine's chest began to heave with sobs. "Why can't you just let me *die*?" Sob. "My sins are too awful. Everyone hates me. I have to pay the price."

Andrew patted the laceration with tissue and mustered a weak smile. "God's seen a lot worse, Jazzy."

She glared at Andrew. "You're still *guarding* me, aren't you?"

Andrew blew out a breath from his cheeks. "Yes, Jazzy, I'm still your Guardian Angel, and John's too, but if I were a human, I'd ask my boss for a raise." He turned to Angela. "I saw the vision of a first aid kit in her luggage."

Angela got up and hurried to the next room. Jasmine sat up and squinched her face. "Who the heck is *John*?"

Andrew reached over and patted her stomach. Jasmine's hand went to her mouth with a chirp. "You *know*? You *named* it?"

Angela returned. "And you might have *told* me she was pregnant. So, this is what this whole thing's about."

Jasmine was sobbing again. It took a moment before she could speak. "They used to stone women for what I did, didn't they?"

With one hand, Andrew put pressure on her wrist wound and placed the other on her head. "You were tricked into this by the whispering demons, Jazzy, and it's pretty obvious you're repentant. Why not just 'go and sin no more,' huh?"

Angela opened the kit and began to clean the lacerated arm with soap and water. "Good thing a nurse always travels with a first aid kit."

Between sobs, Jasmine replied, "Worse than that woman in the Bible, I was about to kill an unborn, too, and another sin besides. I deserve worse than stoning."

Angela was fumbling with a Steri-Strip. Jasmine shook her head. "What do you guys know about first aid? Astringent first. Andrew, you hold the cut closed while she puts on the strips. Next, that gauze pad, then wrap it with the stretchy bandage."

Andrew grinned. "Yes, nurse. So, what's this other sin, huh?"

Jasmine glanced from one to the other. "I thought I would start a new life where nobody knew me. Yesterday I went to this government-sponsored clinic called 'Mother's Choice.' I just wanted to pick up some vitamins and stuff. Before I left, they convinced me to sign up for an abortion. 'It's free in California,' they said. 'Your little problem can just go away,' they said."

She began crying again. Andrew spoke softly. "So, you were planning to go ahead with it?"

"I signed the papers…to kill my baby tomorrow. I did it. I did it, but when I got back here, I realized I don't deserve to live."

Angela knelt over the tub and held Jasmine's head firmly against hers. They cried quietly together.

Andrew spoke in a loud whisper. "But again, you're repentant and you don't intend to kill him now, right?"

She shook her head side to side. "But I was *going to*. Someone like that doesn't deserve to live, does she?"

"Those are the demon words. They know your weaknesses," Andrew declared. "I've seen them whispering to you. Why didn't you pray for forgiveness?"

"'Cause now I'm not worthy to talk to God."

Andrew sat straight up. "Oh dear Lord, those *vile* monsters. That's what they say too, but those beasts have to leave as soon as you speak to the Father."

Angela said, "The words of God will make them go. Then let's all pray together, okay?" Jasmine nodded. Angela took her bandaged hand and Andrew the other. "Dearest Lord, we praise your holy Name. We three beg your presence and your mercy. Listen to these words from Jasmine, your precious child."

Angela grinned at Jasmine, who gave them a weak smile, coughed, and began: "Oh my Lord, I am so sorry for what I have done. I am sorry I have not prayed to you. I do repent. Please have mercy on me and forgive me."

Angela's eyes were closed. She whispered. "And the demons, Jazzy. You remember what to say."

Jasmine sighed but her voice became firm. "You have given your believers this authority: I *cast away* these demons right now in Jesus' name. Amen."

Andrew gave a "yes gesture" with his fist and a wide grin covered his face. "And as an angel of the Lord, I can assure you that you *are* forgiven. Also, you are deeply loved by Him, not to mention us. You feeling any better?"

She nodded and Andrew went on. "All right, then. I'll step out for a moment while you get this silly girl out of the tub, cleaned up and dressed, okay Angela?"

Jasmine's face had become relaxed and peaceful. "So, his name is John?"

Andrew chuckled. "There's a special time for us Guardians. It's when only we and the Lord know about a new human life. It's tradition for us to give the child a temporary name but, of course, no one on Earth knows. Later, the parents decide on a permanent name."

"How do you pick it?"

"I prefer to pick a name with an old Hebrew meaning. John means 'the Lord has shown favor' and from what I can tell, He has given us the favor of one tough little boy. But Jazzy, you certainly get to name him anything you want."

Jasmine managed a weak smile. "No, his name is John."

SEVENTEEN

Jasmine walked between her celestial visitors along the path that edged San Diego Harbor. They each held one of her hands.

"I won't run away. I promise," she said. The angels studied her bland expression for a moment before they let go. Two bicycles approached. Jasmine stepped to the side and placed her hands on the railing. "Look at the size of that ocean. I bet if you guys had your wings and kept flying toward the horizon, you could land in China."

Andrew cleared his throat. "Japan."

She turned to Angela. "Sounds just like a man. He has to be so, so…"

"So accurate. He's like that, but just inhale that clean sea breeze and let it calm you some more."

"It's nice down here, but you didn't have to pay for a cab. There's a bus."

Andrew looked down at her with lowered eyebrows. "We wouldn't want you to have to crack into that ten grand in your purse."

A slight smile broke on Jasmine's lips and Angela released a little squeak and kissed her forehead. "There, she *smiled*. She's coming out of it now, for sure."

Jasmine released a big breath. "I'm really glad you guys came. I was about to do yet another in my series of truly stupid things, wasn't I?"

Andrew nodded. "I'll agree that suicide is high on the list of man's stupidity. The things leading up to it were hasty judgments based on insufficient data, insecurity and lying demons. All preventable if you'd asked God for help first."

Jasmine stood on her tiptoes and looked up at him with a pout. "And I'm getting all this wisdom from a know-it -all Guardian who can't even walk right?" They laughed.

"Sorry, Jazzy. I know I sound like I'm filling out a report but I get that way when I'm trying to control a wave of emotion."

"What emotion?"

"*What* emotion? I almost lost you. We almost lost your precious life."

Jasmine grabbed his hand with both of hers. "Oh, but you saved me, all right. Once you had my wrist, I knew I couldn't move."

"Good." Andrew brought her hands to his mouth and kissed them. "Promise you won't *ever* do such a thing again."

She nodded. "Promise."

He ushered them down the walkway. "Let's walk some more. We understand why you were so upset when Derek's true character came to light, but why run away?"

"My pregnancy. I was just getting over being ridiculed and being a fool for Derek, but now they'd all see me becoming larger each day. I know it's really vain, but I couldn't take it. I wanted to start over somewhere else, somewhere where no one knew me from before."

"But why here?"

"As good a place as any, and I had Mary's letter asking if I could get her car out of impound in Vegas. I also got a fake California driver's License and a new ID in Las Vegas. The hotel here thinks I'm Jessica Tyndale."

Abruptly, Angela stepped out in front of them, turned, and stopped them. "We're missing something, Jazzy. My instinct tells me you've withdrawn into denial of what just happened. Suddenly, you're kidding around with Andrew as though nothing happened. This is way too quick. Less than an hour ago you were trying to kill yourself."

"No, I…" Jasmine gasped, her eyelids fluttered, and her knees buckled. The angels grabbed her before she fell, dragged her to a bench, and rested her head on Angela's lap. As she came to, she began to sob. They waited.

She sat up between them, her breath coming in sobby gasps. Each angel put a hand on her shoulder and waited some more. "You just don't know..." she said. "You don't know how depressed I've been through all this. And then—what I did in that *clinic*." Crying resumed.

Andrew's voice was soft and resonant. "But I *do* know, Jasmine. I was with you the first time you tried suicide, and I thought you understood that's the absolute worst way to avoid life's crises. You found the answer in Jesus, remember? Just trust in Him, and things like hopelessness won't happen."

"You think I'm crazy, don't you?"

"Jumping to wild conclusions based on pure emotion and attempting suicide may be crazy *behavior,* but you aren't insane. Death in all forms is Satan's number one promotion, and so is stealing God's word from your heart. The Lord is anxious to help with your decisions. You just have to ask Him through prayer and reading His word."

Jasmine sniffed and wiped her hair back. "You know what I did in the clinic."

"Of course I know. I was with you, but why not just ask for forgiveness?"

"That paper I signed, Andrew. It was a death warrant for—for John, but I didn't think of it that way at the time. Later, back at the hotel, I realized my child would be lost forever. Better I should die with him. How could a worthless sinner live after that?"

"Jasmine, I want you to know this." Andrew's voice was strained, his face contorted. "First, no lives are lost to heaven. John would live a different life. I just can't give you the details. Look, even if you *had* gone through with the abortion, you would not be lost to the Lord either. He is all merciful and loving. He feels the pain of your wounds and He always forgives a truly repentant heart."

"God could even forgive *that*?"

"Absolutely. He has already forgiven you, Jasmine. You need only to accept His forgiveness. Only then can you forgive yourself and begin a new life, the joy-filled life He wants you to have."

"Really? Maybe my problem is trying to figure things out all on my own. I didn't know I could actually ask the Lord for help. You're supposed to ask? He answers?"

"Yes, and you should also know you had no less than *three* demons whispering into your subconscious. I was outnumbered. Couldn't make them go unless you prayed. I didn't think there was any way to stop your suicide until Angela had this idea and the Master agreed to let us come."

"But I'll have this sin for the rest of my life, right?"

"A demon gave you that lie. I just *told* you your sins are forgiven. What other condemning thoughts were coming into your mind? Let's get them out of you."

"Well, I…" She shook her head. "That I was given one chance to be grateful to God when He restored my legs. I think I only thanked Him once or twice—not nearly enough."

"Nonsense. Anything else?"

"That I'd never be forgiven, and the only noble thing to do would be to die together with my baby."

Angela's forehead fell to Jasmine's shoulder. She muttered, "No, *no*! Oh, those demons."

Andrew declared, "Let's repeat these truths. You're repentant, *completely* forgiven, and God *never* stopped loving you. *No one* remembers that sin." He chuckled. "Anyway, it was some nasty Tyndale woman who signed that paper, wasn't it?"

"Oh, gosh…" Jasmine was laughing and crying at the same time. She hugged her angels. "Thank you *so much*. I'll pray. I'll do better, I *promise*."

Angela held her at arms' length, sniffed in through her nose, and squinted. "So, you're *sure* you are feeling okay now?"

"Oh, I am, for real; I know I've still got things to figure out, but yes, I'm okay. And if I'm guessing your next question, I'm *not* afraid of being a single mother. That was never it, and there'll never be any more craziness with knives. I *promise*."

"All right." Andrew nodded. "Sadness will strike again at some point, but remember, Jesus is always near, and you're never alone. Pray for help if you're feeling blue, okay?"

"Like when I look at the scar on my wrist."

Angela took her hand and gently placed it on the base of her own neck. "I have a scar too, Jazzy. Both our scars are from not listening to God." She grinned. "So you and I have the same reminder."

Jasmine returned a thin-lipped smile. "Thanks…Say, how long can you guys stay here?"

"For a while, but of course, we'll have to go back at some point, but when we're gone, please go to the nearest Christian Pregnancy Counseling Center. They give out love at no charge. Besides that, you'll make friends with other single mothers to be."

Andrew turned them around. "Okay, ladies, let's head back." He pointed. "We can get a cab at that hotel."

Angela walked with her arm around Jasmine's waist. "And while we walk, why don't we talk about your plans for the future?"

Jasmine slipped her arm around Angela as well. "You mean now that I *have* a future."

EIGHTEEN

The next day was Saturday, visiting day at the prison, and Jasmine wanted to see her sister, Mary. Angela and Andrew told her they trusted her. She could go alone. Besides, their fake "angel IDs" might not pass police scrutiny.

Mary was classified as low risk, so they could meet in an open room with tables. Jasmine spotted her bright red frizzy hair jouncing along in the line of inmates as they filed in. Her's was brown and neater, but side by side, they could pass for twins.

Mary skipped over and hugged her sister. "Not allowed," said the guard. Mary turned away from the guard so he couldn't see her sticking out her tongue.

"Wow, it's been *ages*, Jazzy. Sorry that cute doctor broke up with you, but say, you want him hit? I got real good connections in here."

Jasmine chuckled. "I'll bet you do, Miss Contrary. Still the comedian, huh? If you got my letter, you know I brought your car down. I didn't mention it, but I sold mine in Vegas."

Mary gave her an "Ouch" look as they slid into their chairs. "You mean so that you could drive mine down here? I thought you'd come out with a friend. How are you getting home?"

"I was thinking it would be a one-way trip. I uh, well, I tossed the idea of possibly living here. Still not sure."

"Really? But say, I was going to sell my car anyway and get me a cycle. Look, if you want, you can keep my wheels for five hundred under Blue Book."

"I'll think about it. A motorcycle, really?"

"Yeah. I've got a buddy in here. She's like a female Fonzie--talks about her hog all the time. We get out the same week, and she's promised to give me lessons."

"Oh, Mary," Jasmine giggled. "You're such a wild heart. Come see me when you're out, okay?" A puzzled look came over her face. "Say, how the heck did you know about my breakup, anyway? I never mentioned that."

"A couple a months ago you wrote you were dating Derek Marston, and I realized his dad runs some big operation. I got two friends in here who worked for Daddy. After I told them, they let me into their info loop."

"Good Grief, so now the whole *world* knows how stupid I am."

"Yup." She chuckled. "We're all sending it out on the social media."

Mary caught the pained look on her face and put her hand on hers. "Oh, sorry. You know, I try to make a joke out of everything. Seriously, Sis, how's it going?"

"Pretty crappy, Mary, but I just came back to Jesus. With His help, I'm gonna come out of it."

Mary leaned across the table and squinted. "You went back to God a few days ago? Gotta be *after* that bummed out note you sent."

"Well, I..." She grinned. We don't have enough visit time to get into *that* story. Later, I promise."

Mary tossed her hands in the air. "Aw, Sis, just forget that no-good guy. Sure, it takes time, like it took a year for me to get over my husband Bobby checking out on me. Just takes time."

"I know. That was awful. First, the divorce, then Bobby overdosed and died, but then you got an accounting job and moved on."

"Right, and keeping two sets of books for *those* guys landed me in here." She made a face. "They laughed in court when I told them I thought all the companies did that." Another face.

Jasmine smiled. "But, I believe you really did. I can understand why you might think that."

"'Cause I'm a bubble head, right? But back to you, big Sis. You got your legs back now, and your good looks too.

New guys must be after you, and you're doin' that nursey stuff you love. What could *possibly* be wrong?"

"I'm pregnant."

Mary crossed her eyes and belched. "Oops. Bummer. So what're you planning?"

"My first reaction was to disappear and get a new identity so no one would know. A few days ago, I got talked into getting an abortion, and I…" She bit her lip and looked up at the ceiling. "I tried to kill myself."

"Oh, my God, Jazzy. No!" She bounced on her chair, and a scowling guard took a few steps toward them. "You're not *still* thinking that way, are you? Get on your knees and start praying, girl."

"Mary, is that really *you* talking about prayer?"

"Oh, yeah. Most everyone in Yard B got swept away by Jesus and the Spirit. We have our own 'Esther the Evangel' spreading the word. Anyway, God's real, and I *know* He loves you and your kid. You're gonna keep it, right?"

"Oh yes, that part's clear. Remember the angels I wrote you about, the ones that prayed with the others for healing my legs?"

"Yeah, and I thought you'd gone cuckoo bird 'til I got saved myself."

Jasmine grinned and shook her head. "Well, Andrew and Angela burst into my room at the last second just when I was slashing my wrists. They stopped me—saved me."

She lowered her brows. "You sure you weren't dreamin', Jazz?"

"No dream, dear sister. Right now we're all staying in a hotel suite together and running through my cash."

Mary leaned back with a guffaw. "No kidding. And you think *my* life is weird. So, now what are you planning to do with these friends of yours, your personal winged Hosts of Heaven?"

"No wings allowed on Earth, and I don't know how long they'll stay."

"Well, if they leave you, some girls in here really like the support they get in Christian pregnancy centers. They're into giving hope and saving lives just like your angels."

"I'll go, but right now I'm thinking about keeping my new identity, getting a job, and raising my baby here." She searched her sister's face for a moment. "Mary, what do *you* think I should do?"

Mary's eyes went wide. She put her hand on her sister's arm. "Wow, I think that's maybe the first time you've asked me for advice, like *ever*. Look, Jazzy, you know how I've always looked up to my older sister, and I love you, but that's a decision only you can make."

Jasmine didn't reply but kept her gaze level and expectant. Mary straightened up, withdrew her hand, and lightly rapped the table with her knuckles. "I know that you're real sensitive about what people think of you. But okay, for what it's worth, I'd go back to Denver. And if I were you, I'd stand up straight, look 'em in the eye and *dare* 'em to say something."

Jasmine sat quietly for a moment, then reached across the table and covered Mary's hand with hers. "Wow. Now I think I should have been asking your advice all along. You're absolutely right, Mary. That's *exactly* what John and I will do."

"Who's John?"

NINETEEN

When you're living with angels, Sunday is church and prayer day, but on Monday, Andrew and Angela went out exploring on their own. Jasmine caught up with them at Balboa Park. They had been at the zoo, and as planned, she met them at a table in the Art Museum cafeteria. "Hi, guys. How'd you enjoy the zoo? Guess what? We don't have to take taxis anymore. I bought Mary's car."

She slipped into a chair. "That is, if you'll trust me to drive."

Angela grinned. "Of course we do. Look, we ordered you a turkey-avocado sandwich. Should be here any second."

"Thanks. Guess I don't have to ask how you know my favorites. How's your day going, Andy?"

Andrew shrugged, and Angela answered for him. "He's annoyed the animals won't come to him when he reaches out. I keep telling him we ain't in Heaven anymore."

"Like I don't know that." He cocked his head toward Jasmine. "But as your official Guardian, I should be asking: how are *you* doing today?"

"Oh, fine. I threw up this morning, but now I'm hungry. I had to stand in line at the DMV, like *forever*, but I got my car registered with temporary California plates. Lucky I didn't throw out my Denver driver's license."

As the waiter delivered their lunch, Andrew pressed in. "Jasmine, I'm asking…just a second." He reached for her hand and Angela's, said grace, then went on. "I mean, how are you *feeling* today?"

Jasmine spoke as she munched. "Oh, way better. When I think about…" She gulped. "That day seems like remembering a bad dream. Angela, you were so right about asking God to help me with forgiveness, but the hard part turned out to be forgiving *myself*. After that, it was easy to forgive Derek."

Angela gave a 'wind-chime' giggle. "You know, when things like that happen on Earth, we have a little dance number we like to do in Heaven." She grinned. "Course you'll just have to use your imagination."

"Angie, what was that song about love you sang to me?"

Angela's eyes glistened. She leaned toward her, put a hand on her shoulder, and whisper-sang in her ultrahigh voice. "Let His love conquer hate. Let His truth conquer lies. Let His life conquer death."

"Oh, yeah." Jasmine giggled. "You'll get me crying all over again. Say, did you know that my sister came to know Jesus in prison? We prayed together and got reconnected. She's such a funny nut, but I love her."

Angela smiled. "Sounds like you're both reconnected to God, huh?"

"Oh, big time, Angie. I can't believe I got into such a funk. Mary showed me it was all my vanity. She's a lot smarter woman than I ever gave her credit for."

"Vanity's the favorite human weak spot demons like to whisper to. If you ever hear their voice again, give their ugly black wings the boot in Jesus' name."

Jasmine snickered. "Good image."

Andrew was grinning. "This is all so cool." They gave him a quizzical look. "Isn't that what they say? So, Jazzy, have you decided to be Jessica or Jasmine?"

She put down her lemonade, let out a big breath, and tussled her short brown hair. "My little sister also showed me I was being a coward. I was sure she'd want me to stay in California with her, maybe help raise John, but she convinced me to 'get my buns home' and face the music. Mary talks straight up."

Andrew took the check from the waiter and handed it back with cash. "Wow, the day just keeps getting better. You're going to drive your new car back to Denver then?"

"Oh yeah, and I really hope you'll come with me. I'd love the company."

Andrew shot Angela a look. "Angie?" She just shrugged. "Sure, Jazzy. They won't call us back home until God decides, so of course, we'd love to go with you. Right, Angie?"

Angela looked at the ceiling with a thoughtful pout. "Nah. You guys go ahead. I'm gonna stay here and learn to surf."

Andrew returned a slack-jawed, wide-eyed stare, but as her wind-chime giggle began to leak out, he scowled and stuck his tongue out at her. Angela was grinning at Jasmine and pointing to Andrew. "I had him for a moment, didn't I?"

Jasmine grabbed the busboy's arm. "Don't take those. We're not done yet." She filled her mouth with leftover pickles from all the plates. "These taste *great*. Let's order some ice cream for dessert."

#   #   #

Stephen's cell phone rang on his way home from his medical office.

"Stephen? Flynn here. We're closing in on the subject. Got a minute?"

"Hold on. Bluetooth's out. Gotta put in buds—okay, shoot."

"Your lady was using the name Jessica Tyndale, but I said *was*. She dropped that. Checked out of a sleaze hotel in San Diego this morning. But, what do you know? She's back to her real name, visited her convict sister, and bought her car."

"Hey, good. So she's alive and well. So much for your diamond theory."

"Not so fast. This vehicle is an off-road military style, and now she's palling around with a strange young couple. These guys don't match any computer facial profile in the US. I'll bet they're Russian, and I'm sure they're her contact people. I'd also guess they still have the stash on them."

"And I'm sure you read too many spy novels. Can your men talk to her?"

"Yeah, now that she's a missing person, but we'll go in armed. Those bodyguards of hers are likely carrying, so sometimes this can get messy. Just sayin'."

TWENTY

The trio stood in the parking lot examining Jasmine's new ride. "Well, there it is—the typical car choice of my wild little sister. I sell my polite white sedan, and now I'll be driving back in her FJ Cruiser. They don't even make these anymore."

Angela ran her finger along the front fender. "Looks military."

"It's designed to go off-road and has Four Wheel Drive. Mary says I can't live in Colorado and not know how to ski. 'Course the way she said it was: 'Time to break those pretty legs again.'"

Andrew tapped the roof. "So this baby will handle the snow, huh? I hope I get to stay here long enough to start driving."

The angels tossed in their duffels full of the new clothes Jasmine bought for them.

Andrew tapped a large black sack lying on the floor. "Yours?"

"Oh no, that's Mary's stuff. She said I could keep it, all except her laptop. Sh wants that mailed to her once she has an address. Have a look and hand me the Garmin navigator if you see it."

He rummaged inside, pulling out tools, binoculars, and episodes of Entertainment Magazine. He passed the Garmin to Jasmine and held up the computer. "Maybe I can play with this on the way. I'd like to check out the driving rules."

Angela said, "Look at him. He's starting to like your planet now. Best flier in Heaven and he hasn't even been inside a land vehicle before."

Andrew was quick to find the accessory plug in the back and get the laptop running. "Maybe I can even find a simulation of a fighter jet cockpit in here."

The ladies laughed. Jasmine said, "I could stop and give him a driving lesson along the way, but we'd have to find a safe place. Is everyone ready?"

Angela shook her head. "Nope."

"Why? What did we forget?"

"Jazzy, are you planning to just drop in on your friends and yell 'surprise?'"

"Aiee!" Jasmine's hand slapped to her mouth. "Poor Paula and Steve would have a heart attack. By now, they must think I died or something."

Angela pulled out the temporary cell phone she'd bought and passed it to her. "Time to tell them about the 'or something,' right? Paula should be at home now."

Jasmine put it on speaker and punched the number. "Hello, Paula? It's Jazzy. Sorry I ..."

A scream. "Oh, thank our loving Lord! Jazzy, is it really *you*? How are you? *Where* are you? Oh, this is so wonderful."

Jasmine turned to the grinning angels. "I think she's happy." Clearing her throat, she said, "I'm fine, Paula. So very sorry I ran away like that, but I thought I needed to start a new life. Well, I still do, but I'll do it back home in Denver."

"Oh, I can't *tell* you how good it is to hear your voice. Do you know how many people have been going *crazy* wondering about you? All this can't be just because Derek dumped you, now can it?"

"Nah. Course I really hated him for a while, but I forgave him before the Lord and now I feel really calm about it. It's just over."

"Great. That's my girl. But Jazzy, we've got people speculating everything from you living as a hermit to smuggling diamonds. That's all, silly, I know, but still, I sense there's something else. Can you tell me over the phone?"

"Did I—did I mention—I guess I should tell you that I'm going to be a mother."

A quiet response followed a long pause. "I think I would have remembered that conversation."

"I got freaky depressed over it, Paula."

"Look, I understand. You get yourself right back here. You're staying in our guest room, and no argument. My best friend isn't gonna go through a crisis without me. No way. You want me to fly out there? And where is 'there' anyway?"

Jasmine chuckled and smiled at Andrew and Angela as she replied. "That's sweet of you to offer, but I'm driving back with a guy I met in California. He's six foot two and handsome with curly blonde hair—really buff, too. We're gonna practice off-roading in my new RV."

"Okay, that's it. I'm coming for you and bringing a psychiatrist."

"I'm sorry," Jasmine blurted through her laughter. "I shouldn't tease you. It's Andrew. He came and saved my life."

"Andrew? As in *Angel* Andrew?"

"In the flesh, but no wings this time. Angela's here too." She passed the phone to him. "Here, talk to him yourself."

Andrew cleared his throat. "I didn't know she'd do that, but hi. This whole thing is most unusual, but it's true. Angela and I are coming back with her. We'll be there in..." He gave Jasmine a puzzled look, and she held up two fingers. "In two days."

Convulsing in laughter, Paula finally managed, "*Totally* incredible. Why didn't you bring *my* angel too? She-

she, right? Uh oh, I hear wind chimes and I know who that is. Put Angie on, okay?"

With as low and as serious a voice as she could muster, Angela took the phone. "Well, hello, my dear. I'm afraid She-she, or Sheerah's, is not yet qualified for dangerous missions. Paula, I'm distressed to see you've been requiring my man to change poo-poo diapers. Really?"

More convulsions. "Oh, God, I can't wait to tell Steve." Baby cries are heard in the distance. "You guys get here as fast as you can. This'll be such fun. Hear that? Those are my poo-poos calling me. Unfortunately, no Steve in sight."

"Phew-phew. Okay, we're leaving San Diego now. Call you tomorrow night. Bye."

#   #   #

Six hours into their trip, Andrew announced he was concerned about something.

"What, Andy?" Jasmine looked at him through the rearview mirror. "You've been staring out the back window for an hour now."

"That black car's following us."

Angela chuckled. "That's the way it works on earth roads, Andy. Some are ahead, some behind."

"Don't patronize. When we stopped for gas, they used the station across the street, and the driver never took his eyes off us. Tell you what. I memorized the Google Earth photos when we had Wi-Fi back there. We're now passing a big ranch, and the gate's just up ahead. Pull up to it like you were going in and stop."

Angela's head shook. "Really, Andy?"

Jasmine swung into the entrance and stopped by the open gate. "Let's humor him until the car goes by."

The black car pulled over and stopped fifty yards back. Andrew fished out the binoculars from the bag and watched as two men got out. "One's got binoculars on us. They're both wearing guns, ladies."

Jasmine said, "Okay, now you're scaring us."

"The driver took out a cell phone. Likely, he's getting instructions."

"No! What should we do?"

"Stay focused. I'm getting out on this side of the car. Drive through the gate and wait for me. I'll get back in when I've closed it."

As soon as they went through the gate, the black car started up in a cloud of dust. Andrew hopped back in, and they made a cloud of their own. "Go, go!" Andrew shouted.

Angela said. "Won't they follow us in here?"

"Not for a while. There was an open padlock. It's a heavy gate, and I locked us in."

Jasmine glanced back at him. "So, we're trespassing and locked inside some private ranch."

Andrew chuckled. "Well, any sinful trespassing is all on me, but I don't plan on doing any harm in here." He pointed. "Turn left on that farm road. You'll need to slow down."

"Andy, we don't have our direct God connection," Angela pleaded. You're doing this all on your own."

"Wrong. I found out that people *can* find God, but they have to reach out and want it. Anyway, I'm still her Guardian." He leaned forward, put one hand on Jasmines shoulder, and pointed ahead. "You're doing fine, Jazzy. See those cows about to cross this path? Just stop and let them go by. We don't want to hit one."

"B-but aren't we in a hurry?"

"We're safe for the moment. Relax a bit."

A dozen lowing bovines meandered in front of their vehicle. Jasmine let out a big breath. "So, you're saving me again, but from what? Who are those guys?"

"Don't know for sure, but they're not police. I get the sense they think you have something valuable and mean to steal it."

The last of the cow rumps and swishing tails passed by, and Jasmine resumed the slow, bouncy drive through the field. "Any idea where we are going, Andy?"

"In about three miles, this path ends at a perimeter fence. I'm hoping there's another gate so we can get to the County road on the other side."

Angela said. "You keep hoping. I'm praying."

The road ended at a simple bar gate, but it was chain-locked. Andrew got out the tools, pried the latch out of the wood post, and opened it so they could drive through. He screwed the latch back on and hopped over the fence to join them. Angela was nodding. "Okay, I'll admit you are pretty clever, but now your sneakers smell like cow dung."

Jasmine grinned. "He's my hero. Where to next?"

"In about two miles, this road joins a State highway going north and back to the Interstate near Casa Grande. The crooks, or whoever they are, would likely wait for us there. I say we stay on this county road another nineteen miles before getting back on the Interstate."

"You're the boss. You remembered all this from Google Earth on the computer?"

"Yup. Uh, and it's okay to drive a *lot* faster now."

TWENTY-ONE

When Stephen came home, he and Paula rejoiced in the news of Jasmine's return over champagne. They danced around the living room, waking little David in the process. After dinner, Stephen had some calls to make. The first was to Flynn on his private cell number.

"Hello Roger, glad I got you this eve..."

"Yo, Steve! I was going to call you tomorrow. The data's rolling in. I'm about to break your case. Are you sitting down?"

"Yeah, but...listen, I have to tell you..."

"Hold your question a sec. Steve, Jasmine made underworld connections through her sister in the prison in San Diego. She headed out of town with two Russian bodyguards, and I'll bet she's still got that package of diamonds. They helped her evade us in Arizona, but by tomorrow morning, my men should make her location. This time we'll stop her, but then I'll have to call the police."

"I wouldn't do that Roger."

"Sorry, it's my legal duty."

"I'm trying to tell you. There's no package and no diamonds. By any chance, is that 'underworld connection' someone Mary Stearns talked to?"

"Exactly. Mary worked for GPMG associates, and that's the accounting firm busted for cleaning Marston's books, among other things. See how it all fits? Ms Tynan visited Stearns now using her real name."

"Okay if I talk now?"

"Only if you thank me for my amazing detective work."

"Look, Roger, Mary is Jasmine's sister, as you know. She was swept into jail when they did a sting operation on GPMG. She was just working there while she looked for an acting job. Mary is a nutty, fun-loving loon who just got into trouble."

"They all say they're innocent, pal."

"Well, she came to the Lord in prison and is giving Jazzy good advice. That aside, Jasmine is back to her real name for good and driving back to Denver as we speak."

"Who told you that? Mary?"

"Jasmine called us a few hours ago. That 'package' is the baby she's carrying, and the ten thousand was for her to have an abortion and for hush money. She was so embarrassed about the unwanted pregnancy, she thought for a while she'd start a new life rather than tell her friends."

Silence on the line. "Just *pregnant?* She'd go through all that for—okay, I admit, I didn't think of that one. So she got rid of it, huh?"

"Rid? Oh, no. She's having the baby. We didn't figure out what was going on either, but the good news is she's fine, and on her way to stay with us. You can close the case."

"But the…" His voice was hoarse. "The Russians? What about them?"

"They're Andy and Angie, uh, foreigners, but old friends of ours and not criminals. Case closed."

Flynn swore under his breath, then: "There's more bills coming in, you know."

"Okay, document the charges, but no finding bonus."

"There's been a lot of people and a lot of hours. You'll get a fax statement tomorrow, Schwartz."

"You don't sound real happy that Jasmine's safe and well, Mister Flynn."

"That statement won't be the final charge, Doctor."

TWENTY-TWO

Jasmine stood between the two angels as they admired the vast expanse of the Grand Canyon. She leaned against the rail and pointed. "Look carefully at those moving specks down there. It's a train of mules heading lower."

"I'm glad you insisted on bringing us up here, Jazzy." Andrew swept his arm out. "This is as good as 3D gets. In your vernacular, 'way cool.'"

Angela stepped up on the first bar of railing and lifted her arms overhead. "Oh gosh, I just *ache* to swoop down there and soar up on the updraft. Wheee!"

Jasmine grabbed her arm. "No more near-death experiences, please." She turned to Andrew. "Did you know Steve is just dying to talk to you guys about your 4D thing? What's it like anyway?"

"Huh. Words don't describe it. I could write something in higher math symbols."

"Very funny." She giggled. "Try to describe it anyway."

"How's this? If I were taking off to fly this canyon in a 4D world, I could see my flight path and "feel" the future landing place just as I left. Your scientists puzzle over what they call the spooky force at a distance. It's just the 4D world surrounding this one. Simple."

"Forget I asked."

Actually, that flight would be riskier here because I don't see the results of my actions until after I make them. None of you do. Don't know how you live with it."

Jasmine folded her arms on the rail, dropped her head on them, and studied the gravel between her shoes. "So true. Having the future stare me in the face would have changed my life-- never would have gone out with Derek either."

Jasmine sniffed. The angels took the clue and rested their hands on her shoulders. She turned to him. "Tell me, Andrew, when did God know about John?"

His chuckle sounded like a babbling brook. "I think when He created the Earth. What is in His mind will be." He gave her shoulder a squeeze. "But since you are my charge, God told me I had a child to guard as soon as he was conceived."

"So, in a way, he's your child too, huh?"

"I'll say. And a lot of trouble this guy's been, too."

Jasmine turned around and rested her back against the rail. Her mouth began to tremble. "I'm so sorry, Andy. I really am."

"Hey!" Angela stiffened up. "Enough serious stuff." She pulled out a tissue for Jasmine to wipe a tear and blow her nose. "Tell us, Jazzy, is there anything we could do right now to cheer you up?"

"Hmmm. Anything?" Jasmine's face slowly contorted into a mischievous smile. "Okay, I want to hear you both sing, Andy first." She glanced side to side. "Look, no one's around. Nothing to break."

Andrew pleaded, "We might have strong voices, but I'm tone deaf. Can't carry a tune either."

"No excuses, mister. Okay then, just one note into the canyon as loud as you can."

Andrew shook his head, grinning, but nodded. He motioned for her to block her ears and unbuttoned his shirt. She could see his chest enlarge to twice its size. This was followed by a twelve-boat-horn blast that had Jasmine swinging her head and laughing.

"You're next, Angie. How about two bars of 'Gloria' just like you did in the cathedral?"

After a wind chime giggle, Angela expanded her rib cage and sang in two ear-shattering octaves above the range of soprano: "Glo-ooo-ooo-oooria, in excelsis De-eh-oo." All raised waving arms, and she sang it again.

Jasmine jumped up and down and shouted, "Hallelujah." She pointed up in the sky where dozens of birds had formed a tight circle directly overhead. "Look at that! *They* know the sound of Heaven when they hear it."

TWENTY-THREE

Paula put down the phone. "That was my sister, Penny. They just left her place so they should be here in about an hour."

"Why'd they stop there?" Stephen grumbled. "Thought they'd be here by noon."

Paula brought her face in close. "You're as anxious as I am about Jazzy, aren't you? But Penny's kids simply *adore* Angela. She called them to say hello, and they made her promise to stop there since it's on the way. They spent the afternoon with their happy kids."

"Okay, okay. But aren't you going to burn the stew?"

"Ahhh," she giggled. "Now the truth. You're only worried about dinner. It's in the crock pot, and the guest rooms are all ready. Just relax—at least until David wakes up from his nap. You're next up."

Stephen picked up a magazine from the coffee table and fell onto the recliner. "No problem. I'll pretend I'm in my waiting room—probably fall asleep."

"Somehow those kids *know* Angela's an angel. I wonder how. Penny didn't tell them either."

"Really. I just hope they don't announce it in school for show and tell."

Paula giggled. "Too late. The oldest told the class about her last year, including a video of her whisper singing. The teacher said she was 'imaginative'. Penny mentioned it at Thanksgiving, remember?"

#   #   #

Finally a 'toot-toot' in the driveway brought them running out. The ladies hugged, jumped and squealed. While Paula hugged Jasmine, she pouted and said, "You really drove us crazy this time, you bad, bad girl. You're on probation 'til you come clean."

"Yes, *mother*," Jasmine huffed. "Really, I'm awfully sorry."

Paula handed Angela the little blue purse she'd held for her. "It's just like you left it, and I saved a box of your other things, too. Welcome back to human life."

Angela held the purse at arm's length and grinned. "It's still got the 'Jesus Loves You Big Time' sticker on it. I remember we bought it on our first shopping trip together. Of course, I'll have to change the lipstick shade in here. What *was* I thinking?"

Andrew extended his hand to Stephen. "Great to see you again, Steve." He put a hand on Andrew's shoulder and turned him to the front door. "Noisy out here. Let's grab their bags and go inside. They could be a while."

"Sure. I hear your family has grown."

Stephen closed the door behind them. "And any minute you'll hear from our new addition himself."

He grinned. "Paula doing well?"

"Never better. Look, I wanted to ask you in private. How did you manage to find Jazzy, intervene, and convince her to come back? I'm guessing you two didn't bounce in from Heaven just because she was upset about being pregnant."

"You're right. It was a suicide attempt, Steve. Jesus gave us a unique permission to try and stop her, but we had to do it as humans. I'm sure it couldn't have happened without your prayers, though. They made it possible."

Stephen jerked his head back. "Wow, suicide? Wouldn't have guessed *that*. You think there's any more risk?"

"Nah, she's fine and back to abiding with Jesus. She's well aware of the problems in her changed life, but she's ready to face them now. You know her. You must know she is fragile emotionally, but I think she'll be all right."

"Jasmine owes her life to you two. Thanks, Andy. Good work."

"Just doing our job."

"Ahh, you're too modest, but I remember Angela got into big trouble jumping into our dimension to save me once before. You guys gonna be okay?"

"We got permission first. Sometimes God just does things differently. He's sovereign, you know, but as I said, thanks for your prayers, too."

The women came in talking exuberantly. Stephen said, "Here they come. Want to watch a game or something. A beer?"

As Andrew shook his head, Angela and Jasmine came to Stephen to give him welcome hugs. Jasmine said, "I just want to officially apologize for putting you both through all this. And, we're grateful to you for giving us a place to stay, too."

Stephen grinned. "Ah, you guys are family, and all's forgiven—at least it *will* be as soon as Jazzy makes us some of her famous apple nut bread. For now, just get settled. Andy and I will bring your luggage upstairs."

"Oh, I see," Jasmine giggled. "Nut bread. I'll get right on it."

"Say, you should know we did tell the hospital administrator that you're back. Sam, too, but no details, of course. That part's up to you."

Jasmine shrugged. "Uh, maybe I should apply for a job at another hospital."

"Nope. No getting out of it. They didn't fill your position. The hospital has listed you as on sabbatical for personal reasons and wants you to return a week from Monday. You're supposed to go to that HR lady first, though. What's her name?"

She blew out a breath through her cheeks. "Harriet. But if I tell her the truth, she may not want me."

Paula said, "Now, that's a *totally* silly idea."

"It is," Stephen nodded. "Just be matter-of-fact about it. Oh, and Sam tells me his patient, Mindy, is back in the hospital, and she's asking for you. That could be an exaggeration. I'm guessing he'd kinda like to see you himself."

TWENTY-FOUR

Jasmine walked slowly toward the hospital from the parking lot, steeling her psyche for the confrontations she would face when she returned to work. A man was addressing a crowd on a loudspeaker near the entrance. She turned to the side and mingled with the people, knowing, with a twinge of guilt, that this was an excuse to delay going inside.

"…and our County Hospital will have twenty-two percent more capacity," the speaker said. "Yet, with the solar panels on our new annex, we will use *half* the electricity we consumed before. I can take two more questions." He pointed to a middle-aged woman in a print dress. "Yes, M'am."

"Councilman, I notice the Prayer Room and the Chaplin's office are missing from the new plans. Are you eliminating these services after construction?"

"Good question." He grinned. "Bible Baptist down the street has volunteered space for a chaplain for those who feel they need one, and what we used to call the Prayer Room is now more appropriately called the Quiet Room."

"But what you call the Quiet Room is a seven by eight feet and windowless. I'm sure you are aware of the petition circulating to keep a decent sized place for prayer and meditation."

"Sure, but we were able to add two more hospital beds this way, and besides, it's illegal to build a church or pray on public property."

"Praying, illegal? Anyway, councilman, the previous space was *not* a church. We just want a decent space dedicated to the purpose. You can say it's for 'meditation' if you like."

Jasmine thought, *I remember. That's where Steve saw angels comforting people. I think he knew them on a first-name basis.*

Councilman raised a finger. "The new Quiet Room has double insulation. Remember, the separation of church and state is quite clear in the Constitution. Pews and stained glass windows shout out 'church' to everyone, and it is offensive to some." He pointed to a boy in the front row. "Last question now. What is it, young feller?"

"Uh, Sir, I mean no disrespect, but I just did a study on that amendment in high school, and you are mistaken."

"Son, every court in the land knows about the separation. Better ask your teacher."

"The First Amendment prohibits the State from *establishing a religion* like it was in England, but it also *prohibits* the State from interfering with the free exercise of worship by any citizen."

"So you don't know what the word separation means in the Constitution?"

"It's not *in* the Constitution, Sir. Thomas Jefferson wrote a letter to some Connecticut Baptists years after the signing. They were afraid of the State controlling their public activities, and Jefferson assured them they'd be kept *separate* from State interference."

"Look, we don't have time for this." He folded up his papers and stuffed them into his briefcase. "Our courts have rewritten those old laws long ago."

The boy raised his hands and spoke to the departing back. "Sir, I think that's exactly the problem."

#   #   #

Jasmine shook her head. *Maybe I should go right to the prayer room before it gets demolished.* She thought better of it. No more procrastination. *On to Human Resources and face the music.*

She always imagined Harriet "the harsh" as a heartless "nothing but business" type, but the hospital's HR chief seemed glad to see her and even managed a thin smile.

"Harriet, I know I have no right to expect my job back after disappearing on short notice like I did. I'm sorry for the inconvenience I caused, but I guess I had something like a panic attack. I'm better now, and it won't happen again."

She scowled. "Panicked over *what,* may I ask, Miss Tynan?"

"You mean the lively gossip mill hasn't spread the word?"

"Apparently, in this instance, the mill has failed."

Jasmine had a brief coughing spell. "I found out I was pregnant, Harriet."

Harriet's scowl melted like ice cream on a hot sidewalk. She muttered, "That scoundrel. Doctor Marston, right?" She held up a hand. "Wait…wait, not my business."

"So, you see, I could only work a few months before…"

"Oh, that's not a problem—routine procedure for that. For now, we still have your position open. Doctor Wright saw to that."

"So I can return to work?"

"My job is to retain our best employees. After your refresher course last spring, you are certainly one of them." Harriet came around her desk, handed her a paper, and shook her hand. "It's a retroactive permission form. Hope you'll be ready for the morning shift on Monday, Tynan."

"Oh, yes, ma'am, I *will*. Thank you."

Harriet's head shook side to side, and she gave Jasmine a quick hug. "Glad you're back on our team, Jasmine." A lone tear had appeared in her left eye.

Jasmine grinned and turned to the door. "God bless you, Harriet."

Wow. The harsh one is hiding a human inside. She let out a big breath. *I have to admit that going to see Sam is starting to freak me out, but hey, it's lunchtime. Maybe he's out.*

She knocked lightly on his office door and gingerly called. "Sam? Are you in?"

After the sound of a chair falling over inside, Sam flung the door open and embraced her zero point seven seconds after she spoke. He held her firmly in a silent cheek-to-cheek pause lasting well beyond the polite "I've missed you" hug.

Jasmine realized she was enjoying it and pushed away. "Whoa, big fella. Did you think I was dead or something?"

Sam's arms relaxed to his side, but his gaze was intense. "Sorry, I—I never gave up. Never stopped praying." He let out a breath and gestured her toward an easy chair. "Well, how are you, anyway?"

"I'm okay now. Been through a bit of an ordeal, but I'm fine." She sat awkwardly on the chair arm while he half sat on the edge of his desk to face her.

"Well, you look *great,* Jazzy. Want to talk about it? Uh, you don't have to, of course."

"Nah," she shook her head. "Maybe another time. They, uh, they're doing away with the prayer room?"

"Yeah, I'm the one who started the petition to keep it. Look, I understand you not wanting to talk about your leaving, and I won't push for answers. I realize you loved Derek. It must have hurt."

"I thought I loved him—imagined he loved me too, but now I see I was in fantasy land. Childish of me."

"But say, Jazzy, you still owe me that date. Hope you didn't think I'd forget about that, did you?"

"I know, but I…" She slid into the chair and gazed into her lap. "Just feeling a bit dizzy."

"Hold on." Samuel pulled a water out of his small fridge and handed it to her. As she sipped, she realized he was taking her pulse.

He gave her hand a squeeze as he released it. "Sorry if I'm making you nervous, Jazzy. I shouldn't have mentioned Derek. You're probably hungry for lunch. Look, I have some Chinese takeout. I always order big so I can take the rest home."

Jasmine grinned. "This'll probably surprise you, but sure, bring it on."

Samuel laughed, dragged a small table in front of her, and pulled up a chair for himself. He slid the Chinese in the microwave and called, "Fruit juice or diet cola?"

"Juice. Your diagnosis for me is "weak from hunger," right, Doctor?"

Samuel set up their lunch with an unwipeable grin on his face. Sitting down, he enveloped both her hands in his for a simple grace. As he opened his carton, she quickly gulped down two egg rolls and began to work on the shrimp and noodles with the optional fork. Sam lifted his noodles in the air with chopsticks and lowered them into his mouth. "You miss breakfast?"

"Yeah, I wasn't feeling well then."

He cleared his throat. "Getting back to our date..."

"Oh sure, but now there's a great big reason why you might want to change your mind about taking me out. In fact, I don't think anyone ever will."

Samuel cocked his head and returned a puzzled look. "You've got what? Ebola?"

Jasmine put her fork down, swallowed hard, and blew out a breath through her cheeks. "Well, here goes. I'll quote a seventeen-year-old I knew when she announced this same news to her mother: 'I got preggers, Mom.'"

Jasmine tried to keep eye contact in the silent moment that followed, but his look of adoration was too much to bear.

His reply was soft and gentle. "Well, that explains it."

She studied the eggroll crumbs on the table and whispered, "What?"

"Actually, two things, Jazzy." He waited for her gaze to struggle up to his. "First, your appetite, of course, but *especially* your dazzling beauty."

She only returned a vacant stare, searching for meaning.

"What I mean is that in early pregnancy there's a certain aura, like a glow from a woman's face. Perhaps it's the touch of something eternal. I find it hauntingly beautiful."

Jasmine gave her head a twitchy shake. "I don't get it. I've done this shameful thing. I'm even beginning to show, and you actually won't mind being seen with me?"

"I'll pick you up Saturday at six. Try not to be late or disappear for six weeks."

The giggles began despite herself. "Really?! You must be hard up for dates."

Samuel grinned as he cleaned up the lunch remains. "You might have a point there, but now I have to get back to work. Look, I know you don't start back until next Monday, but there's a serious favor I have to ask you."

"About nursing?"

"Sort of. I'm sure you remember Mindy Thompson. She's here in the hospital but due for discharge tomorrow morning."

"Of course. She's Miss 'no more yucky medicine,' and I recall her single mom when she took her home, too. Did Mindy's infection return?"

"Worse than that, I'm afraid. Tests showed her fracture was in part due to bone cancer. It's metastatic and aggressive. The oncologist thinks chemical treatment would only be palliative and cause needless suffering. He just wants to control her symptoms and start Hospice."

Steepled fingers covered Jasmine's face. "Oh, my God. She's such a cutie. You want me to visit her?"

"It would mean a lot to Mindy. She keeps asking about you."

TWENTY-FIVE

Mindy lay in an isolation room, her pale face turned to the window. Her mother sat on a chair beside the bed, body draped across the covers, face resting on her daughter's arm. All was still, save for mother's heavy breaths.

Jasmine walked quietly to the window side of the bed, where she would be noticed. Mindy seemed dimly aware of a presence, but her gaze wandered the room. Jasmine put hands on hips and teased. "Is this my little troublemaker?"

Mindy sat bolt upright, startling her mother, exclaiming, "What?"

Mindy put out her arms. "It's my *Jazzy* nurse!"

They embraced, and Jasmine kissed her forehead. "Hi, sassy girl."

"They said you were gone and wouldn't come back, but I knew they were wrong." Mindy released her grip. "I've got bad cancer. I hope it's not catching."

Jasmine resumed the hug. "No, sweetie, the only thing we catch from you is headaches." She put two fingers on her forehead and swung a pout back and forth. Mindy laughed.

Her mother was sitting up straight. She returned a thin smile through swollen red eyes and cheeks. Jasmine gave her a wiggle-finger wave, "hi."

Mother sighed. "I'm Virginia Watkins. Mindy's chart says Thompson, but I'm her mother. Glad to meet you finally. She talks about you a lot."

Jasmine shot a hand across the bed. "Yes, but I did meet you once briefly. I hear Mindy's going home tomorrow, so I wanted to see her first." She looked at Mindy, dropping her head and voice. "I'm so sorry you got sick."

The child's face scrunched up. "Did God make me sick because I was bad?"

"Oh, *absolutely* not, dear one." She grasped her shoulders with both hands and looked intently into her eyes. "God loves you big time, Mindy. He never makes anyone sick, and I'm sure he's as sorry as we all are." Mindy nodded, squinch-faced.

Jasmine looked back at Virginia. "I don't come back to work until Monday, but is there anything I can do?"

Mindy chirped, "You could come see me."

"And I will if it's okay with Mom." Mom shrugged.

Jasmine turned back to Mindy with a grin. "I know a new finger game, but I won't come and show you unless you promise to draw me a picture. I want a picture of you doing your favorite thing, all right?"

"But Doctor Wright says I can't do those things now."

"Oh psssh," she replied with a flop hand, "you will later when you're well again, but for now, just the picture, okay?"

Mother jerked upright. "Oh, nurse, I don't think you should…"

"Mindy, do you believe Jesus can make you all better?"

"All right, that's enough," Virginia said, speaking over Mindy's "Oh, yes. Jesus can do *anything*."

"Yes, He *can*." She squeezed her hand. "We'll have a fun time soon, but right now I want to talk with your mom." She gestured to the door.

Virginia's scolding began as soon as they walked down the corridor. "Look, it's fine if you want to come and spend some time with her, but it's wrong to put false hopes in my daughter's head. The doctor told me she only has a few weeks left at best."

Jasmine stopped in the hall, made eye contact, and spoke in a quiet voice. "Virginia, do you believe in God?"

"I used to, but what God would take the life of a little girl?"

"Our Lord didn't bring death into this world. We did that when we disobeyed Him, so now we have a fallen world.

But our Lord has boundless mercy and love. Did you know He cured my decade-long paralysis?"

"Mindy said so, but she makes up stories."

"Totally severed spinal cord and in a wheelchair for nine years, but I believed in the power of God like your daughter does. Friends prayed over me, and I just got up."

Virginia's voice became hoarse. "Don't you go giving *me* false hopes either."

"Of course not. Only a few are healed with our best prayers, but the faith of the sick one is important, too. Look, I'm going to talk to those same friends, and maybe we can come over Saturday afternoon. Would that be all right?"

Virginia studied the ceiling in a lip-biting moment. "And what mother could say no to that?"

Jasmine took her hands in hers and grinned. "Tell Mindy she has a play date."

TWENTY- SIX

They all sat around the dining room table finishing Angela's blueberry cobbler. David was on the floor. He sat up and began to fuss. Paula got up, but Angela held out her arm. "Please, let me. After I change him, we'll crawl on the floor together and play a little."

Stephen chuckled. "Hey, let her, Paula. That change counts for my turn."

"Aww," Paula shook her head, "She's spoiling us both."

When Angela left, Jasmine raised a finger. "Could I ask your advice about something?"

Paula gestured, "What? You think you need to ask permission?"

"Well, here's the thing." She pushed away her empty cobbler dish. "But first, I want to thank all of you for saving me. I've reconnected with God, and I'm feeling better. I'm reconciled to starting life as a single mother, and I'm even looking forward to it."

Andrew grinned and gave a little fist shake. "Yeah! But, Jazzy, if you're asking your Guardian for advice, I don't know more than anyone else. It won't be God speaking."

"I understand." She turned to Stephen. "When is that professor coming here? Is it real soon?"

Stephen glanced at his watch. "Not for at least an hour. His plane is just landing. What's on your mind?"

"I can't decide about what to do with the ten thousand dollars in my purse."

Stephen chuckled. "We should all have such a problem."

Paula held up a hand to her husband. "No, Steve, I think she means the money Derek gave her." Turning to Jasmine, "Right, Jazzy?"

"Yeah, Paula. I don't feel right about keeping it. Kinda feels like blood money, but he did say the money was to shut me up and pay for an abortion."

Andrew said, "Have you prayed about what God would like you to do?"

"Sure, but the only feeling I get from His Spirit is that the money's not mine. I could give some of it to charity, or even send it all back to Derek."

Paula squeezed her chin. "What charity were you thinking of?"

"Deeper Still, for women wounded by abortion, and the Pregnancy Counseling Center I'm going to. Maybe the one I went to in San Diego as well. I was still feeling guilty before I went on a retreat with Deeper Still. They really helped me."

Paula's look turned to concern. "With the guilt?"

"Uh-huh. My guilty feelings got all swallowed up by love and forgiveness there."

"Yeah, well," Stephen shook his finger. "Let's first eliminate the option of giving anything back to that creep, Derek."

Andrew cleared his throat. "I don't know if I should say anything that might change what humans do."

Jasmine giggled and imitated a male military voice. "The Guardian of Jasmine Tynan is now permitted to speak freely."

Andrew returned an adoring grin. "Okay. I don't know what you'll think about this idea, but I feel like the money belongs to John. You know, a father-to-son gift."

Jasmine responded to Stephen's puzzled expression by pointing to her abdomen. "John," she said.

Stephen laughed, but Paula said, "That's a *great* idea, Andrew."

"I've got it," Stephen raised a finger. "A College Trust Fund."

"Wait," Paula pointed to Jasmine. "John should tithe and give an offering, don't you think, Jazzy?"

"I do, and I love this idea. I think I'll give twenty percent on his behalf, dividing it between the Centers. Trust fund for the rest." She chuckled. "Committee adjourned."

A baby's screech from the living room caused Paula to get up and run. Angela was on her back, holding David up in the air. Both were laughing. "You guys are having way too much fun in here."

Angela let him down on her chest, and he crawled away to inspect some stuffed animals. "I had no idea how ticklish you humans are." She sat up. "But I think he'll be ready for dinner and a good snooze soon."

The others joined them in the living room. Jasmine announced, "Now don't forget Saturday. I'm counting on all of you to come with me and pray for Mindy."

"We'll be ready," Paula assured her.

Andrew said, "But just before we go, Angela and I want to talk to all of you."

TWENTY-SEVEN

David pounded on the rim of his highchair and sang a few baby high notes while Paula slipped in spoonfuls between his 'words.' "Remember you asking me why we needed a four-bedroom house, Steve? This is why."

"You're right. Even with Angela and Jasmine together in the twin bed guest room, we might need the futon in my study if Angus stays over."

Paula saved a bowl from being swept off the high chair. She nestled it under her short arm. "Don't kid me now. That room of yours looks like it's post-Hurricane Katrina."

"Not to worry. Our Professor will only be here a few hours as far as I know. He's on a stopover on his way to Los Angeles. I promised I'd let him meet Angela, and she doesn't mind as long as there's no needles or X-rays. Couldn't say no after all he's done for me."

Paula wiped David's mouth with a cloth and handed the bowl to her husband. "Okay, here. See if your future scientist will take any more. I'll set up a tray for coffee and dessert. What time should we expect him?"

"Seven-thirty, but I doubt he'll want to use his short time for pleasantries."

#   #   #

Professor McPherson's bright eyes and a silly grin greeted Stephen when he opened the door. "Welcome, Angus, glad you could come. No telling how long Angela will be able to stay here."

"Steve, I feel like a twelve-year-old on Christmas morning. No one will believe me without a photo. Will that be all right?"

"I'm sure. Here, I'll take your coat. Come on in."

He ushered him into the living room where the four stood waiting. Paula strode ahead and shook his hand. "I'm Steve's wife, Paula. It's an honor to meet you, Professor. Steve has told me a lot about you." She turned and gestured. "I want you all to meet Professor Angus McPherson. Professor, this is my friend Jasmine." He took her hand, but his eyes were fixed on Angela. "And, you may recognize Angela from the picture you…"

Angus fell to his knees in front of her, his voice shaky. "You are *indeed* the angel of God. I exalt you."

He was met by "bird song" laughter and Angela's hands pulling him back up. "You silly man. Don't even *think* of worshiping an angel. We are servants of the Lord, just like you. Besides, you humans are the ones given earth dominion, not us."

He looked into her face, transfixed. "But you—you're so *perfect*."

"Oh, there are some," She produced a wind-chime giggle. "Who might argue against that idea?" She put her hand on Andrew's shoulder. "And here's one of them. Andrew is my friend and an angel as well."

Angus gaped at the grinning face and chiseled features looking down at him. Andrew said, "I am pleased to meet you, Mr. Angus." He offered his hand.

"You, both of you? You're *both* from the heavenly dimension? Why did you come here?"

"That's a long story, you see…"

Angela gave Andrew a poke. "And   it's   privileged information."

"Oh, I won't pry. I just want a good look at you."

Paula spoke to Stephen. "Could you get the serving tray from the kitchen?" Then to the others: "Would anyone like something to drink? We have dessert too."

All shook their heads "no" except Jasmine, who piped up. "Do we have any ice cream?"

Andrew opened his arms. "We are not allowed to discuss the details of life in Heaven, but ask me anything else you want."

"May I see your hands?" He examined each one. "Perfectly human. I'm not surprised. Oh," He took out a professional camera from the bag he had carried in and handed it to Jasmine. "Would you mind taking our picture?"

After the photo, Jasmine curled up on the couch with the ice cream that Paula had brought out. Angus stood talking with the angels while the others sat and watched.

"Just tell me this, if you can," Angus asked. "How is it your DNA is so similar to ours, but you don't come from our Earth?"

"Sure," Andrew said. "God created us guardians to serve Earth's humans. He spoke but one word to create us, and called us Children of God. He made you in the same way from Earthly material, but you, er, Adam, rebelled. From that point on, the genetic material of the 'fallen' man remained contaminated with the dust of this Earth and continues to change. You reproduce with this mixture by free choice and so *your* progeny are called the Children of Man."

"So God is hands off now?"

"No way. Christ freed anyone who believes in Him from sin, including Adam. Every person has a special God-given purpose on Earth, and every human life is loved and precious to Him."

"All right, but your DNA in winged form makes you half angel and half human. Why wouldn't He transform you to be completely human when He takes your wings away?"

Angela said, "I think I know. It's a big enough shock for us to lose our wings down here, but if we still have our voice and the same bone structure, it's an easier adjustment."

"For your comfort?"

"I think I'd choke," Andrew stuck out his tongue. "with your tiny lungs."

Angus asked eagerly: "Okay, Angels, I promised no tests, but could I at least have a look at your chest?"

Angela placed her hands over her collar and frowned. Andrew said, "Shirt off?"

"Please."

Andrew displayed his "weight lifter" physique. Angus walked around him and pinched his shoulder. "Are all angels built for strength?" Angela giggled a few chimes.

"Naw," Andrew grinned. "Just the men. We get assigned to move animals around from time to time in the Heaven that's earth-like, and recently I had to pull an angel child out of the river."

Angela said, "Yes, his friends *dared* him to fly across."

Angus grinned. "Sounds like our kids."

"And his wings," Andrew gave a rumbly chuckle. "The boy's wings weren't even as long as his arms. He almost made it halfway, though."

Angus nodded. "Being dared can give you strength. Take a deep breath, please."

Andrew's chest expanded to twice its size. "Hah! Each rib is folded and has an extra joint." Angus snapped a picture, then palpated his throat. "Your larynx is twice our size. Anything else?"

Angela turned her back, and they could see her shoulder blades flapping under her clothes. "There's this," she said.

Angus examined Andrew's back. "Scapulas three times the size of ours and completely hinged. For the wings, of course." He took a photo.

"It's the attachment point, but right now they're completely useless."

The angels allowed Angus to closely examine their heads, arms, and feet. He took another picture of Andrew's expanded chest and checked his watch. "Thank you two for allowing this. I have to get going, but one more question. Your heart rates are very slow, so I imagine your hearts are larger too. Why all this capacity?"

Andrew grinned. "Try flying for a few hours at high altitude."

Angus laughed. "Of course. Last thing. Can I swab the inside of your cheek?"

That done, they all escorted the professor to the door. He bowed, thanked them profusely, and said: "I've made a lifetime study of DNA. If the human sequence were translated into music, it would sound like a combination of rap, ragtime, and static. Angel DNA, however, would burst out sounding like a brilliant, beautiful symphony. Thank you so much, both of you. Bless you." With a grin and a wave, he hurried to a waiting taxi.

The angels waved back. "Via con Dios!"

Stephen faced his friends. "I'm sorry I asked you to go through this, but it really will help us in fighting disease, particularly the genetic ones."

Andrew was buttoning the top of his shirt. "No problem, but in a couple of days, we'll have a try at battling disease a better way. It's late now, but before we go and pray for that little girl, remember that I said we'd really like to give you a, as you call it, a pep talk."

TWENTY-EIGHT

Andrew had given strict instructions for everyone to fast until the afternoon on Saturday and then gather in the backyard for his "talk." He stood on the redwood picnic table facing them, and Angela sat on it, swinging her legs. She pointed to Stephen. "Thanks for hooking us up with hang gliding yesterday. That was wonderful."

"Glad you enjoyed it. Vince's friend, the instructor, said you were natural fliers. If he only knew. Made me laugh."

Andrew smiled at that, then turned to the others and cleared his throat. "Angela has told you that here on Earth, we angels no longer have the direct connection with God we are used to in Heaven. However, we *do* have the same God connection that all of you have. He communicates with you in many ways, but mostly by feelings of being 'called' to do something, and less often with words. This preserves your freedom of choice."

Angela said, "It's still a strong connection, though. You just have to learn how to listen."

Nodding, Andrew went on. "Angela and I both have one of these callings to talk to you about healing."

Stephen said, "Why don't you two just ask God to heal the little girl like you did with Jazzy?"

"Ha!" Andrew stamped his foot. "*That* is exactly the problem. Did you really think that she was healed because a couple of angels were praying?"

Nodding heads said, "Yup, that was it." Andrew looked up at cloud formations with a pained smile. "No, guys, we were only being cheerleaders. We don't have dominion here. It was *Paula's* words."

Puzzled, Paula spread her hand on her chest. Angela pointed to her. "Do you remember what you said?"

"Uh—be healed in Jesus' name?"

The angels grinned. "There you go." Andrew sat down next to Angela. "Apparently, you've forgotten, but you humans have more power here on Earth than you think."

"Power? Us?" Paula chuckled.

"Oh yes, God gave you humans *dominion* over all this Earth and Jesus is your king, but he has delegated His authority to all who believe in Him."

Jasmine put an arm around Paula's shoulders. "*Paula* power."

Angela's finger went up. "Now God does not heal everyone, but faith in both healer and subject is important.

When you pray, don't say something like 'please Lord, heal this person.' Say…" she pointed at Stephen.

"Uh, by the authority given me, I say be healed in Jesus' name."

"Perfect. The words are important, but so is the *heart* of the one saying them. You must truly believe God can and will heal. If you pray in accordance with His will, He is far more likely to make it so."

Andrew called for some backyard prayer and worship time after that. When it was over, he said, "Okay, team, we nominate Nurse Jazzy to take the lead. It's her patient." He jumped off the table. "Let's go. Make it happen."

#   #   #

The mobile home park where Virginia Watkins lived with her daughter had seen more prosperous days. The group walked in from the outside past some lots with overgrown weeds and rusted trailers, but there were sounds of playing children not far away. As they turned onto Mindy's street, they were greeted by a basketball bouncing toward them. Stephen dribbled it back to three teens and almost made a hook shot. One boy grabbed the rebound and dunked it in the basket nailed to a tree.

Virginia had made a valiant effort on the outside of her home. She had fashioned a stone garden with flower pots on either side of the walk, and her front door was recently painted a light blue. After a light knock, she met them and hugged Jasmine. She whispered, "Thank you all for coming. I think Mindy's sleeping."

Jasmine replied, "Glad to be here. I think you know Doctor Stephen Schwartz. This is his wife, Paula, and our friends, Angela and Andrew. How's our girl been doing?"

"Not well. She started having seizures yesterday and can't walk. Doctor Wright put her on something for them, but it makes her sick." She ushered them over throw rugs and a creaky floor to her daughter's tiny bedroom.

Mindy was propped up in her bed, awake but groggy. She didn't move or smile when they walked in, but gave them a little wave when Jasmine introduced them. Stephen came around the other side of the bed with Paula. He took her hand and said "Hi" with a smile, but his look was pained. He noted she had labored breathing and the pupil in one eye was fixed and dilated.

Mindy raised her head and pointed to Angela and Andrew at the foot of her bed. "Angels," she whispered.

Jasmine asked, "Now, how can you tell that?"

She looked past them at her mother standing in the doorway. "They're angels, Mom. There's a fuzzy glow all around them. Am I dead now?"

Virginia hastened to come closer and stood between them. "Of course you're not dead. Look, I brought a whole *bunch* of angels to pray for you, Dear."

Mindy shook her head. Her voice was soft and croaky. "No, just those two." She made eye contact with Angela. "Right?"

Angela grinned. "Yup, you nailed us, sweetie, but we're just Guardians here to help if we can."

Mother nodded. "We're all here to help you, Mindy."

Jasmine took her other hand in both of hers and held it firmly. "Mindy, first, do you want to get well, and do you believe God can heal you?"

"Yes, I do, and Jesus can do anything. I know it."

"He sure can," Jasmine smiled. "And we are His ministers here on Earth. Keep your thoughts on Jesus, Mindy." She placed one hand on Mindy's head and the others extended their hands toward her. "Dearest Holy Spirit, by the authority you have vested in me, I ask that you dwell now in this, your precious child. I declare Mindy's healing *now in Jesus' name.*"

Mindy twitched, and Jasmine released her. "How do you feel?"

She lay quietly for awhile. "Real tired," she whispered. "Nurse Jazzy, can I sleep now?"

"Of course." Jasmine grinned and kissed her forehead. "Dream about Jesus who loves you big time."

The group gathered outside the front door, and Virginia thanked them all for coming and caring. "The oncologist said she could go at any time now, but at least you tried. Mindy was glad to see you, and I'm happy about that."

She ventured a thin smile and said with a wink, "You even brought angels."

TWENTY-NINE

The slender, tuxedoed waiter bent down to Jasmine. "If you will not have dessert, perhaps you would care for some espresso and dark chocolate?"

"Uh, no thanks, but I'd like some regular coffee."

"We have Sumatra Dark, French Roast, and Latte."

She giggled. "Okay, that last one."

Samuel said, "I'll have one too." The waiter bowed and shushed away.

Jasmine scanned the mahogany paneling and Victorian trappings around her. "Sam, this is an amazing restaurant. Sorry, I ordered appetizers too, but they were all delicious. Thanks."

He gave a fake pout. "Not to mention downing half of *my* cocktail shrimp, but of course, you're eating for two."

Jasmine relaxed against her chair back and studied his face. "Mind if we talk candidly for a moment?"

"Oh, Jazzy, I'd welcome it."

"Well, I guess I've known you for seven or eight years now."

He grinned. "I remember those early wheelchair days. You had just received your nursing degree, and you wheeled into the Surgicenter, determined to earn your own way."

"But I had put the idea of being involved with a man out of my head. I admit to being flirtatious at times, but everyone knew I was just kidding. I knew no one would respond."

"I did."

"And at first, I thought that was pity. I also thought you were married, but then I heard your wife died years ago. I turned down your invitations 'cause I thought you were way out of my league, as they say."

Samuel leaned forward, his eyes narrowed. "More likely the other way around. I want you to know I never pitied you. In fact, I very much admired your spunk and cheerfulness despite your handicap. When you entered a room, there was an aura of—of *goodness* that came with you." He chuckled. "Yeah, from the moment you wheeled in, I knew there would be laughter. You seemed to love everyone."

The waiter returned with their coffees and Samuel asked for the check. Jasmine nodded. "I do love to be with people, but I never dared to think of any relationship with you outside of work. You weren't just older, you were well respected. I'm just some ditsy girl, and back then I couldn't even walk."

Samuel's look of total adoration returned. "Oh, Jasmine, you are far, *far* more than that. You may be fun-loving, but you are bright, insightful, and a woman of God."

Jasmine's lip started to tremble. She looked away. "If that's true, why have I been stupid, careless, and sinful?"

"Ahh, the soul slips up a lot. That's not your spirit, the real you. Look..." His cell phone sounded. "Oh, sorry. See, this is what you'll have to put up with if you're going to hang out with a doctor. Be warned. They aren't supposed to call me except for an emergency."

He put the phone to his ear. "Yes, this is Doctor Wright...She *did?*...and she's in the ER? Send her for a stat Cat Scan and admit her, my orders."

He pocketed the phone. "It's Mindy. She's fallen and hit her head. She may not have long to live, but I don't want her to die of a concussion tonight. I can call you a cab, but I'd like you to come with me. Will you?"

"I'm with you, Sam. She's my patient too."

THIRTY

Samuel and Jasmine hastened past the chaotic Saturday night emergency room. Jasmine tried to run but stumbled in her unaccustomed high heels. Samuel grabbed her before she went down. "Come on, they've given Mindy a private room, fourth floor."

Mindy's mom, Virginia, met them in the room. Guilt covered her face. "Doctor Wright, I only left her for twenty minutes. She was sound asleep, and I was tired from work. I took a shower and changed, but when I came out, she was sitting on the front step. I saw her bleeding forehead and I remembered what you said, so I picked her up and drove her straight to the hospital."

"That was the right thing, Virginia," Samuel asked. "Do you know how she fell?"

"No, I told her to be calm and kept shushing her to keep quiet. She kept saying 'but mom,' but I made her keep still." She clasped her hands together. "Thanks for getting us out of the emergency room, Doctor. They took her to X-ray."

"Wait, you're saying she made it outside. Was she still wearing pajamas?"

"What difference does that make? I know I should have asked my neighbor to come in and watch her." She covered her face. "This is all my fault."

Jasmine put her hand on Virginia's shoulder. "No, it wasn't, and the doctor just needs a little history. Was she in her pajamas?"

"She was in her play clothes." Virginia sniffed. "Oh, blood was running down her cheek. I'll *never* leave her alone again."

Samuel said, "Dressed and outside, huh? Anyone else around? Anyone see her fall?"

"No one in sight, doctor. Thank you both for praying for her, by the way. Sorry it didn't work."

"She's in an X-ray gown now, I assume. Those her clothes on the chair?" He picked them up. "Yup, blood spots on the right shoulder. Ah, and there are grass stains on these pants. Is there a lawn in front of your house?"

"No, but we have a community park two blocks away. She must've been in one of those better moments if she made it that far, huh?"

"I should've mentioned that the seizure medication also relieves pain. That's a benefit, but it could give her a false sense of well-being." He glanced up. "Ah, here she comes now."

Mindy propped herself up on her elbows as the X-ray tech wheeled her in on a gurney. The tech grinned at her mother. "Here's your Miss Wiggles." He released the strap holding her, and she quickly rolled over onto the bed.

Mindy waved at those around her. "Hi, Doctor Wright. Hi, Nurse Jazzy."

Samuel peeked under her forehead bandage. "You seem amazingly chipper, young lady. Alright, Jazzy will..." He snickered. "I mean, *Nurse Tynan* will ask you about what happened to you." He pointed down the hall. "I'll go check your X-rays. Be back in a minute."

When the doctor walked away, Mindy crooked her finger so Jazzy would bend down to listen. "He really *likes* you, you know."

Jasmine laughed. "And you knew that before I did. Well, guess what? We were out on a date when we got called here."

Virginia said, "She's *always* playing 'Miss Matchmaker'. I think she's suggested six different men that I should get to know."

Jasmine gave Mindy a squinty face. "And how many boys' hearts have *you* broken?"

She sucked her cheeks in. "There are three boys who like me and *two* boys in love with me, but they're all way too immature."

"I'm sure." Jasmine chuckled. "Well, my assignment is to find out what naughty thing you did to get your head banged up. So, spill it. What happened?"

Mindy flashed a worried look at her mom. "Okay, after you healed me, I got really sleepy."

Virginia added, "You were asleep, so I thought it was safe to leave you, but you were talking in your sleep."

"I was talking with Jesus, Mom. He said, cause I believed Him, He made me well. He also said he loved me." She saw her mother's puzzled expression. "Wasn't a dream, Mom. *Real.*"

Jasmine patted her arm. "No argument there, but how'd you bust your head? Was it because you couldn't walk straight?"

"The kids outside were playing 'catch me if you can' so I got dressed and ran out to join 'em. Jimmy Prescott chased me up a tree and out on a branch. He's one of the ones who likes me, and he was trying to grab my arm. I slipped off and scraped my head on the branch, but I landed on my feet. Didn't hurt *nothing*."

Mother was holding her hand over her mouth and crying. "Oh, Mom, I'm okay. It was just a *scratch*, but when the boys saw the blood, they ran. Don't cry, Mom."

Mother embraced her child and spoke between sobs. "You look so well, I...I want to believe too."

A shout from down the hall startled them. "Miracle of God!" The shouter kept repeating it, getting closer and closer. "Miracle of God!" It was Samuel. He appeared holding up an X-ray in each hand.

Doctor Wright stopped at the foot of Mindy's bed, looked at her, and whispered, "Miracle of God, Mindy."

He held up the films for all to see. "This needs to be shouted to the world. Look at this." He wiggled one skull film containing two white blotches. "Metastatic cancer, like tennis balls in the brain." He wiggled the other one. "This is today, only one week later. Cancer's all gone. I mean *non-existent*."

Virginia embraced her child, raining kisses on top of her head.

Samuel smiled at Mindy. "You're all well, my child."

What could they all do but laugh—and cry—and laugh.

Mindy held up her hands. "I've been trying to tell you."

THIRTY-ONE

Back from the hospital after their date, Jasmine and Samuel pulled into Stephen's driveway and stopped. She flopped her head back on the headrest, exhaled through puffed cheeks, and smiled. "That was one heck of a memorable first date, Sam, and it all began with such peace and elegance, too."

He turned his body sideways to gaze into her face. "Aw, I feel we've been dating in a way for years. True, it didn't seem elegant when we madly rushed out to a dying patient." He reached out a hand for hers. "However, it is unbelievably elegant to discover Mindy wasn't dying but was cured by God's grace through your prayers. One reads about things like that, but I've always had a tingle of doubt about those accounts."

"God has a purpose in those He heals. He often says: 'So that you will know I am the Lord.' We have an awesome, prayer-answering God, don't we?"

Samuel quietly massaged the hand he held for a moment. "And He's already answered one for me."

She giggled. "But it seems that I can't run off-balance in high heels thanks to my new weight distribution. Thanks for catching me."

He pointed to Jasmine's abdomen. "You can still do most things with your added front load. Unfortunately, running isn't one of them. But, wow..." He looked up and shook his head. "That joyful look on Virginia's face; I think I'll treasure her expression forever."

"But how about Mindy's: 'What's the *matter* with you guys. I *told* you Jesus made me well.' I just love that sassy girl."

"Faith comes so naturally to children. No wonder Jesus loves them so. Look, I can't resist witnessing this to my congregation tomorrow. Want to come?"

"Yes, but could you hold off till next Sunday, Sam? Two very special guests of ours are leaving, and Paula and I want to take them to the service at our church. We're having a going-away party for them after, but say, I'd love it if you'll come with me."

Sam chuckled. "Like you think I'd say no?"

"It's settled, then." She opened the car door. "See me to the front door. Paula's probably peeking at us out here like we're a couple of teens."

They found a space near the door and away from the windows to enjoy an embrace and a long, intimate kiss. Sam cupped her face in his hands. "No matter *what* else happens, Jazzy, this one will go down as the most memorable day in my life."

Jasmine lightly touched the tip of his nose, a twinkle in her eye. "Wait until you meet my friends tomorrow." She chuckled. "You might change your mind."

THIRTY-TWO

Stephen and Paula were the first of their group to arrive at church with David cradled in Stephen's arm. Liz and Bill were the door greeters, and Liz, who had seen the two of them first meet there for the first time, winked at them. "My, what a fine couple you are."

Stephen angled a thumb, pointing to a side door. "Amazing things happen in your bible study."

Liz laughed, bent over, blew David a kiss, and gave Stephen a sideways hug. "I know, and believe me, you're not the first."

Everyone was delighted to have Virginia make her first trip to church in a long while. Together, the group filled up an entire pew, including Mindy, who didn't want to be sent away with "the children." Instead, she wriggled in between "her angels" to their delight. Her mommy moved next to Angela "just in case." Mindy had embarrassed her in the past. She was inclined to stand on the seat, sing with the music, and wave her hands in the air.

Jasmine arrived, hand in hand with Samuel. She asked Stephen, "Where's Paula?"

"She'll be back in just a sec. She's getting David settled in the nursery."

Jasmine looked down the row. "Looks like the angels are having a great time with Mindy. I see the offering envelopes are quickly becoming artwork."

Samuel spoke quietly in her ear. "Angels? You mean those people who came back with you from the coast?"

Jasmine wrinkled her nose and giggled. She held up a finger. "I'll explain later. Promise. We'll talk before the party this afternoon."

As soon as the band began booming out "How Great Is Our God," a winged angel slid out of a portal and started dancing on the same big rafter Angela had used at Paula's wedding. Only a few could see her, of course.

As the congregation stood, many with uplifted arms, no one noticed that Stephen and Mindy were pointing up. Paula said, "You see one, don't you?"

"Oh, yeah." Stephen nodded. "Fuzzy outline, so she's still attached to the portal—a young woman like Angela, but with black hair—in fact, she's a black woman. Wow, what a funky dance."

Of course, the pew angels and Mindy, who now sat on top of Andrew's shoulders, could see her too. Mindy squealed in delight and tried to imitate her motions. "Look, Angela, she's *pointing* at me."

"That's because she's celebrating your healing and your mother's, too."

"But mother's not sick."

Virginia leaned in. "You talking about me?"

Angela turned to her. "Oh, sorry, I meant your accepting Jesus—spirit healing. I guess you can't see her, but a happy angel is dancing on that crossbeam and being even sillier than I was."

Mindy was now wiggling and thumping her shoes on Andrew's chest. She waved. "Look," she said. "She's waving back."

Angela said, "Can we tell her, Andrew?"

"Sure, why not?"

"Mindy, that angel's name is Ophelia. She goes by "Opie."

"Oh, no, look." A great hand reached out across the beam, grabbed Ophelia by a wing, and dragged her fluttering back into the portal. "Angie, someone pulled her away."

"That's 'cause—" Angela gave a wind chime giggle. "'Cause she's so happy she's being naughty—broke a Council rule to say 'Hi' to you. You see, Mindy, Opie's your personal Guardian Angel."

THIRTY-THREE

Stephen and Paula's backyard was a typical grass rectangle backed up against a hill and with somewhat neglected border shrubs. It offered a view of rolling hills to one side, yet remained private. They had set up a party table on the cement patio by the house. Paula and her husband busied themselves bringing out food, a beverage, an ice chest, and a coffee pot. "Steve, are you sure we should have invited Virginia and Mindy to this? It'll be enough of a shock for Sam, but who knows how those two will react."

"Darlin', I'm shocked every time myself, but if it goes as expected, they'll treasure the memory. On the other hand, if our angels *don't* get called back, at least we'll have a nice party."

"Steve, Angie said their call was for sometime this afternoon, hopefully not before the others get here. Oh, and bring out the mixed nuts. She likes those, and there's fresh lemonade in the pitcher on the kitchen table."

Stephen headed back inside. "You worry too much. Angie said they give some kind of signal when their ready."

"Wait, Steve. Should we let David see this? He might be scared."

Steven stopped at the kitchen door, turned around, and raised a scolding finger. "Paula, stop worrying."

"Okay, okay."

As he went in, Angela was opening the door for Virginia and Mindy, and they were receiving warm welcome hugs. Stephen recruited Andrew to help him carry out the provisions.

As soon as they walked into the backyard, Mindy did two cartwheels on the lawn, ran to the newly assembled swing set, and began swinging aggressively. Paula said, "Steve, you told me you weren't sure about the stakes holding that down."

"Yeah, see, my plan was to bring in an innocent kid to test it for me." She stuck her tongue out.

Virginia was chatting with Angela and Andrew. "Everyone here is convinced that you are really angels from Heaven. I'm not saying I doubt you, and I know angels are in the Bible, but showing up on Earth as people? Isn't that rare?"

Stephen stood behind her. "I wish it *were*. These guys just keep dropping in on us all the time. It's really annoying."

The angels laughed. Angela pointed at Stephen. "And of all the humans I could have been assigned to, I wound up protecting *him*. So glad we're finally getting outa here."

Stephen worked his way between the two and put his hands on their shoulders. "And this handsome dude on my right is Jazzy's guardian. Seriously, Virginia, neither of us would be alive today without these guys."

Virginia glanced over at her daughter. She was now trying to swing high enough to bounce the seat chain. "Okay, assuming you two really *are* angels from Heaven, how do you go back? Do you disappear or what?"

Andrew replied, "In this form, Virginia, we have to be taken back by someone in contact with the dimensional portal. Heaven is in a separate four-dimensional universe, but it surrounds this one."

"You sure you're not promoting some sci-fi movie?"

Samuel and Jasmine walked in, Samuel noting, "That would be fun enough, Virginia, but Jazzy tells me we're gonna see some great special effects."

"All right, then." Andrew stepped back on the lawn with Angela and raised his voice. "Now that we are all here, Angie and I would like to say a few words before we have to leave."

Angela gestured for them to sit. "Grab some lemonade and pull the patio chairs around. We'll take questions in a moment, except we can't talk about the details of what Heaven is like."

"First of all," Andrew began, "I want to thank all of you for your hospitality. For all the training we've had about the hostility here on Earth, you have made our time with you a pleasure. My guess is we were kept here long enough to make sure Jasmine was well past her dark time, coach you all in how to pray, and perhaps to do some teaching as well."

"And it was great," Angela said, releasing a "chimy" giggle, "to see Jazzy doing her own healing prayer. We all thank the Lord for healing our dear Mindy."

Andrew continued. "But we're called to talk about another serious matter before we go. We have angel colleagues serving persecuted Christians in the Middle East and elsewhere. Satan wants to wear out the saints so they give up. Their angels are under *real* stress, but they can better serve their charges when you give your Christian brothers and sisters prayer support. Please remember the persecuted every day. It will make a real difference."

"Yes, the *Devil*," Angela pounded her delicate fist on her knee. "and his Demons are very active on Earth today, but he only gains dominion here when people *give* it to him. Humans surrender their rights when they give in to his temptations."

Andrew dropped his voice and pointed a finger. "Satan thinks he can have control of the Earth forever if he eliminates all those who worship the true God of Abraham,

Isaac, and Jacob. By 'eliminate' I don't mean just killing. People also fall under his dominion if they either have no God or worship a false one."

Angela turned to Andrew. "They may miss an important point, though." Her arm swept over her audience. "Satan's clever and his subtle attack is to slowly change what was once the worship of God into a manmade creation. These are dead churches masquerading as righteous ones. They brag about their 'good deeds,' and proclaim a 'new' understanding of God's word, but they change its meaning. They boast about their tolerance and coexistence."

Andrew's head hung low. "Tolerance of evil and sin. Sadly, so many humans are deceived by these churches, even if their leaders sincerely feel they are well-meaning. They no longer seek to abide with their Lord Jesus, and yet a truly righteous path would be so easy for them--so full of joy. We wish all humans would invite the Holy Spirit to live within them. That would change everything."

Samuel leaned toward Jasmine and whispered. "You sure these friends of yours aren't pastors?"

Jasmine shook her head. "Nope. Pay attention. You'll see soon enough."

Angela nodded. "You see, Satan delights in the 'pew sitters' who don't realize they are following the traditions of *men* and not God. They have no idea they sit in 'shiny whitewashed tombs.'"

Paula raised a finger. "But we win in the end, right? Jesus will come in glory to rule the Earth and the faithful."

Andrew shrugged. "Well, yeah, but we do not know how many faithful will remain. If the Devil fulfills his plan, there may be none left. Presently, he is using a false religion and convincing his converts to kill everyone who follows the one true God. He hopes the only ones left on Earth will be those who either join them or deny God's Word."

"Well, that's a bummer," Stephen said. "You guys used to be a lot of fun."

The angels grinned, and Angela spoke up in her squeaky voice. "But the *good* news is that the faithful can completely defeat Satan and his strongholds."

"And not with better bombs," Andrew added.

"No," she added. "Our weapons are not carnal ones. They are mighty through God to pull down the evil strongholds. The real war is in heavenly places against the hosts of spiritual wickedness, and God answers your prayers. He responds by bringing legions of angels to our side—*big* ones. In fact, you're going to see one of our giant warriors any minute."

Mindy came hopping between them, bouncing a "stars and stripes" beach ball. She left it on the lawn and ran to her mother. "Why is everyone so serious?"

Virginia drew her close. "Shhh, your angels are telling us important things before they have to go."

"No!" She ran to Angela who sat on the picnic table and grabbed her dangling legs. "Oh, don't go, Ms Angie. Can't you just stay with us? You like it here, don't you?"

Angela picked Mindy up and sat her on her lap. "You are so right, but we don't have a choice. Andrew and I will never really be far away though, and I'll bet you spot us from time to time."

Mindy pouted. "But that means you're going back to Heaven, right?"

"Yes, but listen to Andrew. He's about to tell us what's going to happen next."

Andrew was smiling down at them but turned to the others. "We don't want to startle any of you who haven't seen this before. In a moment I will signal for a portal to open beside me. It will look like a swirling white light about my height. Please do *not* approach it." He pointed at Mindy. "Especially you. A large angel will be coming out."

Angela slid Mindy to the ground. "He's nothing to be frightened of, but he'll appreciate it if you look scared until he speaks."

Mindy said. "I won't be. I *like* angels. Do they have toys in Heaven?"

Angela drew her in close again with a wind chime giggle. "No, Dear. Just watch, okay?"

Andrew raised his arms and suddenly there was a whirring, screeching sound. The portal appeared beside the picnic table, silent, but swirling and surrounded by white light.

Mindy pointed. "Angie, does that go to Heaven?" Before anyone could stop her, she ran over and threw the ball into the portal. It disappeared.

Virginia ran forward and pulled her daughter back with the others. "I'm *really* sorry," she said.

In a moment, a sound like a distant buzz saw came from the portal. A nine-foot white angel popped out and spread his wings. His voice was low and resonant. "Do not be afraid. I come in peace."

Paula and Stephen raised their hands and opened their mouths in mock terror. The huge angel looked down at Angela. "They're not even a *little* scared, are they?"

"Well, Saul, you might have been more frightening if you weren't carrying a beach ball in your arms."

Angel Saul's chuckle resembled a motorcycle starting up. He looked around and tossed the ball at Mindy. "Yours, I presume."

Mindy heaved it back at him, and they bounced it between them a couple of times before Mindy ran to him and hugged his giant leg. Saul went down on his haunches, and they did a knuckles hello. He looked up at Angela, still sitting on the table. "Maybe it's more fun not to be scary. You guys ready?"

"One more minute." It was time for final hugs and goodbyes.

Finally, Saul put his arm around Angela and Andrew and picked them up like luggage. Angela called out to everyone as they approached the portal. "May the Lord bless you, each and every one. We love you."

Saul bent over and walked through the portal which closed behind him with a snap.

The silence seemed profound. Samuel broke it with, "Like *wow!*"

Jasmine grinned up at him. "*Told* you they were real." She noticed a camera in his hand. "You didn't."

He chuckled. "I did."

Mindy pointed to the table. "Mommy, Mommy, Ms. Angie forgot her purse."

Lying by itself on the picnic table was a small blue purse bearing the sticker that read: "Jesus loves you big time."

THIRTY- FOUR

Mindy stood, clutching the purse to her chest, her face scrunched up in 'pre-cry.' "Angels are all *gone,* Mommy." Virginia went to her and drew her close. "It's all right, baby. They had to go home. Maybe they'll come back again one day."

"Angela forgot her purse. Can't we find her?"

"No, baby. I'm sorry but I don't think she needs one in Heaven, and besides," she released her and chuckled, "I doubt that visitors are allowed."

Mindy held up the purse to where the portal had been hoping something would happen. With this, Jasmine and Paula came over. "She did take it to Heaven one time before, Mindy," Paula said. "But they don't need earth things there. I keep Angie's purse with her clothes so we'll have them for her if she comes to visit again."

"She'll come back." Mindy nodded. "I know she will."

"Come on inside. I hear David stirring. I could use your help with him."

Mindy brightened and handed her the purse. "Okay, can I carry him somewhere?"

Heading for the house, Virginia shot Paula a "can't believe that worked" look.

Stephen and Samuel stayed put in their chairs while the ladies busied themselves inside and Samuel handed over his phone with a grin. His pictures included one of Saul in full wing extension, beach ball and all, and one with an angel under each arm part way through the portal. He chuckled at Stephen's look of amazement. "What? Did you think my pictures would be blank or something, Steve?"

"No, and they're just great. You're taking them to the TV news team I suppose."

"No way. They'd add 'making up a hoax' to my threatened suspension at the hospital."

"What? You're kidding. Suspended for what?"

He laughed. "Apparently running down a hallway shouting 'miracle of God' is not considered professional behavior. Who knew?"

"Really?" he chuckled. "Don't you get a hearing?"

"Yeah, Wednesday."

"Just tell them the truth. You've got the X-rays. Anyone would be excited, and besides, you've been like a rock in a stormy sea at that place. Everyone respects you."

"Thanks, Steve. They're not going to suspend me, but I won't have any new patients until the hearing. The board had to have some response to the complaints. You're right. I think I'll bring them Mindy's X-rays and let 'em judge for themselves."

"Sam, her story should make national news headlines."

Samuel nodded his head. "Sure, but only the tabloids will touch it. The most you can expect is a Christian documentary one day for the unbelievers to scoff at. But the good news is that for a few days I'll have more time to see Jazzy."

Stephen leaned back with a grin. "Man, I can't tell you how happy it makes Paula and me to see you two together. She told me Jazzy has had a crush on you for years. Darned if I get why she went for that creep instead."

"It's complicated, but I'm just glad we have a lunch date when she's off on Friday. I'm trying to be cool about this, Steve. Don't want to scare her away, but I guess you know I love that woman like crazy."

He chuckled. "Oh, yeah. I think we guessed."

Mindy burst out the back door, kicked the beach ball, and did two cartwheels. The last wheel flubbed, and she fell behind the picnic table. The men stood up, trying to see what had happened to her. She let out a piercing scream, and they all ran to her, mother and Paula blasting out the screen door behind them.

As they slid around the table, they found Mindy sitting on the grass, laughing. She jumped up, holding a crème colored feather almost three feet long. "It's *Saul's*," she announced. "Can I keep it, Ma?"

Mother stood, open-mouthed. "I, I don't know. I guess it's up to Doctor Schwartz."

Mindy was skipping around and swishing the feather overhead. Stephen said, "That sure is a lot larger than Angela's."

Paula pointed. "She's already got the base of it dirty. Look."

Stephen motioned for Mindy to bring it to him. "Wow, this is huge. Okay, you can keep it on one condition. I need to snip off some samples first."

Mindy began to leap around the yard, her prize wafting through the air, now like a wing. Paula said, "And just what are you going to do with those pieces?"

"I'll send it to Angus with Sam's photo. He'll be ecstatic."

"You'd do that for free?"

"Course not. I'll expect center court seats at the next Duke-UNC game."

"I'll pass on that, but it will be so nice for you."

He studied Paula's scowl. "*And* I'll contribute to the Pregnancy counseling programs in North Carolina?"

"Very thoughtful of you."

Stephen grinned through gritted teeth at Paula's unchanged scowl. "And, *and* I'll ask him for a week at his rental house on Holden Beach."

"Now you're talking."

THIRTY- FIVE

The Toyota FJ whined and growled up the twisty mountain road, Jasmine exuberantly spinning the wheel through the turns. They hit a pothole, bouncing Samuel to one side. "Oof, I thought it was cute of you to pick a place for our date. Now I'm not so sure."

"Hey, you said you wanted to discover the 'real' me."

"But..." The four-wheeler bounced and lurched. "When do I get to know where the heck you're taking me? It's not ski season."

"Almost there." She giggled. "You're used to being in control, aren't you?"

"Yeah. This is a first. So, I'm seeing a new side of you, right?"

"Maybe so. I think I'm channeling my sister, Mary, today. This is her old car. I see why she liked it."

"Really? You never mentioned her. Where does she live?"

The FJ squealed and bounced through a tight curve. "State penitentiary near San Diego."

Samuel became quiet. Jasmine glanced toward him. "Surprise," she said. "Mary got caught up in her boss's crime. She'll be free in less than two weeks now. She's the only family I have."

"Will she fly out and visit you?"

"Who knows? If she does come, it's more likely she'll cruise out here on the new Harley she's buying."

Samuel laughed. "This keeps getting better. Mary's in a motorcycle gang?"

"Not yet, but she said she'll join one. Wait 'til you meet her, Sam. She's the funniest woman I know."

"What's the name of the gang?"

"I think she said…" They had reached a plateau with houses and shops. Jasmine slowed and pulled up to a large green wooden building. "She said it's called 'Ride on King Jesus' or something like that. Well, here we are."

"I can hardly wait to meet her." He looked up at the sign over the door. "Oh, Cliffhanger Restaurant. I've heard of this place."

Jasmine put the stick shift in reverse and cut the engine. The FJ shuddered to a stop. "This little settlement is an artist's colony. Half of this building is a gallery, and Paula has some of her paintings on display here."

Samuel got out and looked around. "Nice funky place. I changed my mind. It's a good pick, Jazzy, but how's the food?"

She locked the car with her key. "Don't know. I just came to enjoy the art last time. They say it's great, though, and wait until you see the view of Denver from the back patio."

Samuel hastened over to her, slipping his arm around her waist as they went up the stairs of the porch. "Well, you're in charge of this date. Do we do anything besides eat?"

"Sure." She shook her red hair. "After dinner, we can browse the art gallery, maybe get our picture taken, and walk around the shops."

Inside, the hostess greeted them in a print dress that reminded him of Little House on the Prairie. Jasmine had reserved a window table. Samuel moved close to the glass, shielded his eyes, and peered down. "Ahh, you're right. Fabulous view, Jazzy."

The hostess asked for a drink order. Jasmine opted for a cola, but Samuel said, "Make mine a glass of Chianti. I'm not driving."

While they ate, they were treated to the spectacle of three hang gliders showing off outside their window. When they caught the updraft, the gliders swooped and turned, sometimes almost touching the deck outside.

After dinner, they wandered through the outside shops selling 'tourist trophies.' Samuel bought a hand-carved picture frame for their selfie picture before they returned to the main building to appreciate the art gallery.

Jasmine pulled him by the hand to Paula's section and gestured to a picture of a smiling woman in a wheelchair waving a wooden spoon aloft. "Me," she said.

Samuel put his arm around her shoulder and drew her close. "You didn't have to tell me. You cook?"

"My mother was a sous-chef and I cooked for Paula and myself when we were roommates."

"Good grief, now you've moved up to the most perfect woman in the world."

She giggled. "Hardly, but I'm glad you think so." He enjoyed her shy smile and batting eyelashes.

Another painting showed an angel dancing on a church rafter with a wedding going on below. "That is Angela, of course. It's from our description of her at Paula's wedding. Naturally, no one would suspect the subject was a real live angel."

"The face is perfect. Of course, she didn't have wings when I met her."

Jasmine 'squeegeed' around in his arms to stand against Samuel. She looked up at him. "So, since you're picking our *next* date location, how about giving me a teensy hint of where that might be?"

He grinned and lightly stroked her cheek. "It will be somewhere familiar, yet it will be a new perspective—a shelter yet fully open."

She produced a squinty pout. "Oooh, sounds like one of those dreams in the Bible. You're such a man of mystery."

Samuel gave her pouty lips a quick kiss. "And *your* choice after that?"

"No mystery. After what you said, your 'perfect woman' will be cooking dinner at your place."

THIRTY-SIX

Paula shouted over the TV in the next room. "Steve, could you turn that off?"

"Just a second!" Silence. Stephen appeared at the door to the den with a pained look. "What is it, dear? They just kicked off for the second half."

"Professor McPherson's on the phone for you. He sounds excited."

"Oh, good. I should remind him of his beach house offer, right?" Paula grinned and handed him the phone with a thumbs up.

Stephen stretched out on the den couch and sighed. "Hi, Angus. What's up?"

"Hope this is a good time. Sounds like you're watching a game."

"No problem. I put it on record so now I'll only miss the ads. Tell me; is Saul's DNA any different from Angela's?"

"It is, and I have something spectacular to tell you too. But first, Saul's not human. He may *look* like a big person, but he is a pure genetic creation like Angela. His DNA has some *similarities* to human beings, but he's built like a fighting machine."

Stephen chuckled. "I'm not surprised. You should see his forearms. Saul looks like his dad was an oak tree."

"So, I assume he's one of those fighting angels the Bible describes."

"Absolutely, and the only type described as appearing to humans. The Guardians call his type 'Class One,' but when little Mindy ran up to him, he turned to sweet mush."

Angus chuckled. "I won't even ask about seeing him in person. I know the answer."

"Right, but he's spectacular, huh? I hope this means we get that week at Holden Beach in September?"

"Sure, but if you knew about the *other* thing you sent me, I would have given you the *deed* to the beach house just to have the privilege of analyzing it."

"What? I only sent you clippings from Saul's feather: the quill tip and a few vanes."

"Vanes with dried blood on them."

"So, the feather was torn off. Were his blood cells interesting?"

"Steve, it wasn't his blood."

He thought for a minute, got up, and began to pace. "Really? Some other person?"

"Not a person, Steve. It's from an alien creature. I presume Saul fought with it."

"Oh, now I remember. Angela said she got him to clean his wings. He'd fought with a demon, a fallen angel. Is their DNA much different from the good guys?"

"Yes and no. Its *sequence* is angel-like, but here's the spectacular part. The demon, if that's what it is, isn't even carbon-based like every creature on Earth. He's a *silicon* life form. No such thing on *our* planet, Steve."

"Oh, my God." Stephen swung around and plunked down on a chair arm. "Silicon life forms really *can* exist?"

"Living and bleeding."

"Well, I hope you don't think you're gonna examine a live one of those in my living room." He heard Angus laughing. "But, say, if the Bible's right, they were once angels. Why do you think God would exchange all their carbon atoms for silicon?"

"Do I know the mind of God? Maybe it's because when they're dead, no earthly life, plant, or animal could come from the demon remains."

"So, no practical value here, huh?"

"Well, if I had to guess at another use, I'd imagine silicon creatures could live in a high-temperature environment."

Stephen walked to the window, his tongue poking out of his cheek. "Yeah, good idea. I think I know the toasty place a demon might call home."

THIRTY-SEVEN

Several angels sat on two branches of a banyan-like tree facing each other, their wings draped behind. Andrew was speaking. "Thanks for taking the time to come, everyone. I know you are all busy with your charges, but since our Earth responsibilities overlap, I think updating each other will help us all."

With a nod, Angela said, "Yeah, things keep changing, don't they? Say, I don't see Paula's guardian, Sheerah. Did you tell her about this meeting?"

"Sure. Maybe she's just late. Remember, she's also got little David to watch as well. Meanwhile, how are things with Stephen?"

Angela giggled. "Oh, just great. He's close to the Lord now, a loving husband and, well, at least he *tries* his best to be the perfect father. We've been through so much together, and looking back, I realize I've grown in understanding as much as he has."

"But it must be a bit easier on you now that no one is trying to kill him."

The murmuring giggles of the angels resembled a babbling brook. "Just a bit. But it's not all trouble-free. No human life is. One of his patients is doing her best to seduce him, but with my help, he's doing a good job keeping her at arm's length."

"Great, and Jasmine has been a story of both tragedy and joy this year. Remember that even in good times, calamity can be sudden. The best defense is always to remind your charges to stay close to the Lord and His Word. It's really the only way humans can cope with their world." He pointed to a burly, dark-haired male angel on the opposite branch. "Wouldn't you say so, Justin?'

"Oh, yeah, and without Him, how could they learn patience?" He gave a quick wave to the others. "I'm Samuel Wright's guardian, if you didn't know. He's had his sights on one special woman for an entire Earth decade, and he's never wavered. Sam's got more patience than I do. Oh, look. Someone's coming this way."

A small female angel was making labored strokes, flying just above the surface of the river below. As she flew up to their tree, she struggled to gain altitude and finally collapsed on the branch. Another angel had to grab her so she wouldn't fall. Andrew asked, "You all right, Sheerah?"

She shook her slack face at the others. "Thanks, just exhausted is all."

Andrew said, "She's Paula's guardian, and I guess, little David's too, right?"

"You guess? You know why I'm late? The little guy crawled behind a couch, found an ant trap, and thought it was a lollipop."

"Is he okay?"

"I think so, but I had to scream into Paula's ear and distract David at the same time." She searched the faces around her. "Say, if anyone's charge is being pursued by a hit man, I'll switch with you. I almost pulled an 'Angela' this afternoon."

Angela was laughing. "And don't you *dare* do it, guys. Dropping into Earth's dimension has more consequences than you could believe. Sheerah, have you gone to the focus group for infants?"

"Sure, last week, but I got called away for a David emergency five minutes into it."

"What's so hard about infant care?" Andrew asked. "I'll have one of my own to look after pretty soon."

Sheerah was shaking her head. "Ouch. Ask for a transfer right now. David's just walking. He heads for open stairwells every time."

Angela fluttered over to her branch, sat beside her, and put her wing around her shoulders. "Oh, She-she, you're a nervous wreck. I could help you when Steve is home from work. Just call me."

"Good, cause yesterday David discovered the backyard. Do you know how many things he found to eat out there?"

"Yeah, but I got you beat, Sheerah."

The comment came from a diminutive angel woman with Asian features. Andrew said, "Meet Rebecca. She's called Becka, and she was Mindy's guardian in her early years."

Sheerah raised her hands. "You got worse than that?"

"Mindy was just past her second birthday when she disappeared from her locked house for six hours."

"But she's fine now. What happened?"

"I've saved that kid's life half a dozen times. First, you should know, she has a one-sixty IQ, and second, she's felt the presence of God since birth. If I dare to peek out of my portal for a second, she waves at me. It's just not right."

Sheerah said, "Well, that sounds like a plus to me."

"Really? Mindy feels the need to minister to others, but her social *experience* still matches her age. Trouble, huh?"

"Her house was locked?"

"Here's what happened, and I wished I could have pulled an 'Angela' on this one myself. Well, her mother, Virginia, was still married and living in a suburban house at the time. Mindy was in the living room looking out over the street while her mother was in the kitchen. She heard a dog barking in a yard across the street and decided she'd go and see what was bothering him. She then proceeded to figure out how to unlock the front door. One-sixty IQ, remember."

Rebecca readjusted her branch position to face the others. "Picture this. There goes this two-year-old waddling down the front walk and heading for the street. I darn near jumped out of my portal and grabbed her right there. Instead, I whispered 'look' when a car approached and 'stop' when there was danger. Mindy did hear me and made it across the street okay."

Sheerah said, "She was heading for the yard with the dog?"

"Right, and this dog was a Rottweiler who had severely bitten intruders before. I was yelling 'no, no,' but this time she climbed the rail fence anyway and dropped into the neighbor's yard."

"Did the neighbor see? Did anyone?"

"Nope, the neighbors were gone. When Virginia realized Mindy had disappeared, the police and volunteers combed the neighborhood. I should mention Virginia's husband said he was too busy at work to come."

"But if she was in the yard across the street, why didn't anyone find her?"

Rebecca laughed. "When the neighbor came home hours later, he was surprised to find his dog looking out of his dog house and not coming for dinner. He was even more surprised when his Rottweiler growled at him when he came near. Fortunately, the dog house was hinged for cleaning and he tipped it back. Mindy was sound asleep with her arms around the dog."

Andrew chuckled. "So Mindy was comforting a lonely dog, and he was guarding her."

"Exactly, and needless to say, she got 'dog visiting' privileges, and Virginia made new neighbor friends. As Mindy grew up, she would talk to people in wheelchairs, entertain the feebleminded, and help anyone in trouble. She was more of a comfort to her mother than the other way around when her daddy left them. But my favorite story is when she stopped a bully from beating a boy in second grade."

"She fights?"

Rebecca giggled. "No, she *befriended* the bully. Strange, huh? Fearless. Well, she talked to him about how they both had broken homes and why there was no point in taking out the anger on others. She told him about God's love, and this actually changed the bully's attitude. The two of them began helping others. I love Mindy just awful."

"Wow, I get your point." Sheerah nodded. "But now she's Opie's?"

"Council thought I was getting too stressed. They reassigned me to a man in a nursing home. I would have stayed with Mindy, and I still check up on her, but how about that *healing*, huh?"

"Spectacular, and right to the point of this meeting," Andrew said. "We're getting to know each other's charges so we can help out with them when needed. Keep talking."

Sheerah looked at him with squinted eyes. "Andy, your charge is going to deliver soon. Are you going to ask for a woman to take over?"

"No way. I'm staying. Yeshua won't tell us about the future, of course, but He did hint that my special talents would help John one day."

"What special talents?" Angela frowned. "The only one I know for sure is you're the best flier I've ever met."

Andrew turned to Angela and grinned. "Roger that."

THIRTY-EIGHT

"I don't think a walk in this particular park is such a good idea, Sam. I've got bad memories here."

Samuel gripped her hand more firmly and began to swing it back and forth. "But, darling, that's exactly why we *should* come here. It's the best therapy to destroy all those nasty thoughts left in your head, Jazzy."

"I see, so this is therapy, Doctor?"

"Well," he guffawed. "I guess in a way, but more than that, I'd like it to become your favorite place all over again. Do you know about the gazebo on the far side of the lake? It's out on the end of a dock."

Where was he going with that? She looked up and studied Samuel's large, gentle face. "Paula did a painting of that dock, but I never rolled my chair that far."

Samuel pointed. "There. It's just coming into view, and we're in luck. I think we have it all to ourselves."

"For what, pray tell?" Suspecting he was planning something, her grin showed a glint of impishness.

He chuckled and returned her look. "Why, for the *view,* of course, and perhaps a place to talk. Take courage. I'm carrying some dessert in this bag. It's your reward for walking this far with me."

"Good. I might not be in condition for power walks, but you've probably noticed, I'm eating like a fullback."

At the dock, Jasmine released his hand and briskly made for the pink and blue gazebo. "Oh, it's so pretty, Sam, and look, there's a picnic table inside."

She went to the far railing, held on to a support column, and rested her slightly protruding abdomen on the rail. "You're right. There's a super view from here. I love the way the mountains tower over the city."

Samuel caught up, placed his hands on the rail, and stood beside her. "Ah, Jazzy, I'm feeling so good right now—a little nervous, but good."

"Really? In ten years, I've never seen 'Mister Rock of Gibraltar' nervous."

"Well, I am." He studied her twinkly eyes and admired the freckles on her nose in the sunlight. "It's 'cause I picked this particular time in our lives and this particular place in our great universe."

Samuel went down on one knee and took Jasmine's hand. She gasped. "Jazzy, you must know how deeply I have loved you, and for *so* many, many years. I am asking you today: will you be my wife?"

Jasmine gazed down into his pleading eyes for a terrifyingly long moment. "Oh, Sam, you know I'm in love with you, too. How could I say no?"

He pulled out a ring box from his pocket and almost dropped it. Samuel stood up and laughed nervously. He opened the box and pulled her hand across the picnic table. "With my hands shaking, I hope I don't drop this in the lake."

The ring was a perfect fit. They embraced and enjoyed a long kiss in the sunlight, the puffs of lake breeze rustling their clothes.

"Come on, Sam." She pulled him toward the shore. "Let's not eat until later."

As they walked arm in arm toward the lake path, Samuel said, "Darling, I'm thinking we shouldn't have a real *long* engagement."

Jasmine giggled. "And I'm thinking about three weeks."

"But a real minister."

"Absolutely, but just some family and close friends."

"Our churches might not be available on short notice. Off the top of your head: where would be your first choice for our wedding?"

Jasmine stopped him and turned him around, a mischievous grin covered her face. "I know *just* the place. Please, oh please, don't say no."

"Whatever you want, my love. I'd say yes to anything, well, maybe not the top of Mount Telluride, but anything else."

She giggled. "I want to marry you in our hospital prayer room."

His eyes grew wide. "Uh, I understand the lift chairs go almost to the mountain top," He coughed. "And maybe we could get Ski-Doo's to go the rest of the way."

"No, seriously." She wiggled in against him. "We met in that hospital, and we still work there. It's perfect for a small wedding, don't you think? Besides, it should make a statement that the Hospital Council can't ignore."

Chuckling, he shook his head as he soaked up her enthusiasm. "*Totally* against the rules, of course. Actually, I love it, but we can't ask permission. We'll have to just drop in there and do it."

"Preemptive strike." She opened her hand as if dropping a bomb. "Phissh, boom."

They turned to continue their walk. "Who's your Maid of Honor? Your sister, Mary?"

Jasmine laughed. "Not on your life. She'd have the bridesmaids wearing pink polka dot pajamas and leather jackets."

"Can't wait to meet your incarcerated family."

Abruptly, Jasmine stopped and stepped in front of Samuel, a sudden frown on her face. He blurted out, "Uh, just kidding."

She spoke through gritted teeth. "It's not that. I know you were, but I just had a huge guilt pang."

"Guilty? Why?"

"Sam, have you really thought this through? If you marry me, in a few months, you'll be cuckolded into raising someone else's kid. Honest," She bit her lip. "I'd *completely* understand if you want to leave our relationship just as it is."

Samuel grasped Jasmine's shoulders, comforting her pained expression with a steady grip and resolute calm. He had never been eloquent in choosing his words, but in that moment, Samuel produced a declaration that released a gusher of laughter and tears: "My precious Jasmine, my forever love, please listen to me. From the very moment we become man and wife, Johnny will become, and will forever be loved by me. He will always be my child."

PART TWO

TWENTY-THREE YEARS LATER

All the days ordained for me

Were written in your book

Before any one of them came to be.

PS 139: 16

PROLOGUE

Angela was getting out of breath as she flew higher and closer to the mountains. She also wished she'd worn a warmer jacket, but this is where Andrew was performing for the contest, so she kept her wings resolutely stroking higher into the purple sky.

There they were. Between two snow-capped mountain peaks, she found the cluster of angels flying in a large, slow circle around the challengers. One bearded angel was performing wild flips to the cheering crowd. She joined the circling watchers as the announcer called out: "That was Angel Peter, number twenty-six, in his final flight, performing a double Immelman reverse. Next up is Angel Andrew, seventy-seven."

She thought, *Hope I can pry him away to come back with me after this*. Andrew was climbing higher and higher in a tight upward spiral to prepare for his turn before the judges. Almost out of sight above them, he suddenly folded his wings and plummeted like a bird of prey. As he passed through the circle of onlookers, he began spinning rapidly, then checked his dive with outstretched wings and hurtled back above them. He descended in a spiral staircase, making flying cartwheels look easy.

Andrew climbed again and finished the run with barrel rolls that flipped in changing directions back to the starting place amid shouts and whistles from the appreciative audience. He had won yet another contest. Finally, the angel audience began a gentle glide down to warmer altitudes.

Angela tried to flap over to him, but she had to wait for two lady fans who were layering on their sugary compliments. When one left, she slipped in beside him. "So, this is what you mean by 'time with the boys,' huh, Andy?"

He laughed. "Hi, glad you came. Women can compete too, you know." He gestured to the woman flying on his other side. "Heather, this is Angie, a long-time friend of mine."

The women exchanged tiny waves and forced smiles. Heather said, "Isn't Andy just *amazing*? I don't think anyone has ever done that last one…like ever."

Angela turned her head to Andrew and did a quick barrel roll. "He learned that spiral thing from old Greyson, but he does run the stunts together well."

Andrew chuckled. "Okay, Angela, I'm guessing you didn't come up here just to watch me win a trophy."

"Right. I'm hoping you can join us to hear the special news release this afternoon. Rumor is that the changing things down on Earth are coming to a head."

"Things are *always* changing down there, and anyway, they'll rebroadcast to our quarters tonight."

Angela played her trump card. "I happen to know Archangel Michael will be there."

Heather's mouth became a giant oval. Andrew nodded. "Well, it must be important, then. Sure, let's go." He turned to Heather. "You want to come with us?" She responded with enthusiastic nods.

#   #   #

The trio looked down as they approached a canyon bounded by cliffs on both sides. Angels were arriving from all directions. Angela pointed. "We're going to be just in time. My friends reserved a ledge near the cliff top."

Andrew grinned. "In that case, lead the way, Angela."

"If you insist." She pointed her wings overhead, flipped on her back, and plunged straight down, spinning like a touchdown pass. Heather did a straight dive just trying to keep her in sight, but Andrew copied every move.

Angela snapped her wings out to brake her dive at the top edge of the cliff, Andrew right behind her. "Nice flyin', angel girl. You should try next year's competition."

She laughed. "I just do that for fun."

Heather exclaimed, "Ooh, look. The Class Ones are taking their seats along the top."

Angela waved. "There's Saul." A wing shook back in reply.

"And, if I'm not mistaken," Andrew said. "I can see Michael himself approaching."

"Oh, oh, let's hover." Heather panted. "I want to see him up close."

After they had indulged their new friend, they settled down on the reserved ledge, and Angela introduced her to Sheerah, Ophelia, and the others. "We have a few minutes before the broadcast. How about everyone gives another quick update on our charges? Andy started this idea years ago, and I think it's really helpful."

Andrew grinned. "Ha, so that's why you got us all to come together. Okay, I'm now with John Wright, son of Jasmine and Samuel. He's engaged to be married and a test pilot in the Air Force. God helped Angela and me save him from dying from an abortion, and I've always felt the Lord has a special mission for Johnny and me. He won't tell me, of course, but I'd guess it has to do with this flying we both love so much."

Angela gave him a doe-eyed look. "Whisper any *suggestions* to him, Andy?"

Andrew pointed at her but spoke to the others. "She knows me, but I've kept most all my nudges to straight guardian stuff. Of course, I've been tempted to do more: like when he almost forgot to switch his fuel feeds last month. He could 'a stalled his plane at thirty-five thousand feet. I feel like Johnny's my buddy, but at least I never played matchmaker like you, Angela. How's Steve doing, anyway?"

"Fine. Well, boring, but that's good. He's a great husband and father. Heather?"

"Me? My charge is Chang Woo. He's eleven, and his family has to keep their Christian faith a secret from the Chinese authorities. I whisper lots of encouragement and try to warn him if the enforcers are close by. Wish I could do more."

Ophelia pointed at herself. "You guys got it easy. You know about that Mindy girl? Our dear Lord healed her cancer, but she's too smart for her panties if you ask me."

"I'm Opie, by the way." She grinned at Heather. "Her mom's guardian is Esther, but she's not here. Mother Virginia met this real estate developer in her church singles group, so smarty-pants Mindy got to go to all the best schools. She could've had scholarships anyway, that one."

Angela asked, "Last I heard she was getting her PHD, but where is she now?"

"Teaching cosmology at Cal Tech and showing how a superintelligence is behind the creation of the universe. She was suspended and sued at her previous College for suggesting there was a God."

"There was a court trial?"

"Yeah, an angry atheist student saying any mention of God was proselytizing. Mindy won, though." Opie chuckled. "I liked the part where she explained to the judge that cosmologists are just searching for the cause of an explosion. She said, 'If a bomb went off in the city, would you eliminate the possibility that someone set it off?' The judge laughed and dismissed the case."

Angela ruffled her wings. "But what about her colleagues? They might not be so easily convinced."

"Some of them are upset. They hate the idea of someone older than humans and more intelligent than they are, but they can't disprove Mindy's equations. She's even nailed down our four-dimensional universe surrounding theirs. Smart woman, huh?"

"Never doubted that. What else is she up to?"

"Mindy volunteers for a children's hospice, where she likes to arrive in an angel costume and pray for their healing. Guess where she got that idea?"

"Still single?"

"She lives alone, unless you count her big Rottweiler. She's so busy she hardly goes out, but I know at least three men who'd like to break that streak. Anyway, I'm off her case next month. Yeshua is assigning a smart, sassy young angel to take my place. Name's Susie."

"*My* Susie?" Angela giggled. "Oh, she's a perfect match. You and Susie keep on nudging her in the right direction, okay? Mindy is like family to me and my human friends. I'm sure you know they've kept in touch. And that brings us to Sheerah?"

"Well, if I had to live as a human, I'd be Paula. She's so caring, and she tells everyone about Jesus. Besides that, she's really great at ministering to the disabled, and she's an accomplished artist. Be with her for a while and you'll be *thanking* God for any disability you might have. She makes disabled people feel God made them that way so that they can minister to others and serve the Kingdom in a special way."

"So cool. And finally, Ruth?"

"I got stuck with Jazzy after Andy dumped her so he could buddy up with her flyboy son." They laughed, and Angela clonked Andrew's head with her wing.

"No, seriously, Andy did the hard work with her, and I'm grateful. Jasmine still has her happy, frivolous side, but also her sad, 'Is this all there is?' times. Fortunately, she's mellowed into a great mother and wife. Three times a week, she works at the Pregnancy Counseling Center, and she goes to retreats with Deeper Still, where she helps women wounded by abortion. Still, you never quite know what she might do next, but I'll admit it: I do love hanging out with my Jazzy."

A deep, low hum began in the valley below. Ophelia asked, "Does anyone know what this special news bulletin is about?"

Heather had her shoes off and was dangling her bare legs off the edge. "Big troubles on Earth, I heard. Hope it's nothing evil."

The holographic image of a huge angel began to emerge in the canyon, even while late-arriving angels flew right through it. He appeared to be standing on the valley floor, but his eyes were level with the top of the ridge, making his height about a quarter mile.

"Blessings and greetings from the Most High," his voice boomed. "I bring news that will affect everyone here on Heaven and on Earth."

Ophelia nudged Sheerah and whispered, "Anyone *not* just get a nervous chill?"

"At this very moment, Satan is making his big move to conquer the Earth, beginning with all Christians and God's chosen people. He fears the revival brought on by the prayer warriors now spreading over the Earth, and feels he must strike immediately if he is to win." The angel hologram pointed a great wing toward the Class Ones. "Is Satan going to win?"

The deep resounding "NO!" knocked rocks and some more petite angels off their ledges, leaving them to flutter back up to their places amid the echoes in the canyon.

"This battle will not just be a carnal one for the Children of Man, but will be fought among the powers and principalities in these high places. Hosts of Heaven, are you ready?"

This time, the angels below hung on for the gigantic, "YES!"

"As we speak, Satan has ordered his deceived carnal forces to attack the Holy Land, but we angels are supported by a great surge of prayer strength from the faithful. Praise the Lord!"

"Praise the Lord!" they all shouted.

"Every guardian must be armed against demons and ready to whisper support to your charges. You are ordered to carry your short swords and bucklers on your person at all times. Stay close to your human and listen closely for God's word.

"The United States, like Israel, was dedicated to God, but over the past half-century, Satan has corrupted every mountain of their society. He has won battles to corrupt government administration, education, finances, the arts and media, and even the churches themselves.

"Just as he used the Persians, Assyrians, and their terror in ancient days, the Evil One has sent them back to destroy God's people. Under his deception, they believe their false god has ordered them to kill or enslave everyone in both Israel and America. After that, they will feel empowered to destroy everyone who does not bow to their god. Finally, Satan will turn them on one another so that only a handful of his followers will remain. He hopes this will prevent the return of Yeshua." He pointed to the cliff top. "Will he succeed?"

"NO!" They thundered back.

"No, he will not, but there will be much suffering on the Earth before his defeat. Each of you will listen closely for your Lord's instructions, and remember, God will abide with humans and angels for all eternity. Hallelujah."

All the angels shouted, "Hallelujah!" The image extended both arms and wings and bowed to the angels as it slowly faded away.

THIRTY-NINE

Dover AFB,
Officers Club lounge

Two soldiers in fatigues and military haircuts carefully studied the next shot on the pool table. John Wright's bright blue eyes squinted along the cue. His shot just grazed the target ball.

David Schwartz called, "Number seven, corner pocket." Click. Clunk. "Number two, side pocket." Click. Clunk. He grinned at John, who rolled his eyes at the ceiling. "Great to have you visit our base, Johnny. Didn't I see your aunt on a movie poster?"

"Yeah, Mary Stearns. After all those years in TV comedy, she got a serious role, but I'll believe it when I see it."

"Number nine, corner." Click. Clunk. "Did I mention that my shoes have to shine right down to the soles? And, of course," He chuckled. "Get your shoe polish out, Johnny. Number four, corner pocket." Click, Clunk.

David took a winning, grinning pose, his pool cue resting on his foot and holding it out to one side like a medieval knight.

"All right, you win, but I think I've been hustled."

"Johnny, you know my mother has beaten me, and she only has one arm."

"Yeah, and because of that, she gets to use a cue rest. But as I recall, the last time she won, you were eight."

David chuckled. "Okay, I'll assuage your sore-loser angst and buy you a beer."

John scowled at him as they left. "Obviously, you refueler pilots have too much time on your hands." When they slipped onto barstools, John added, "I can't even have that beer right now because my squadron is on alert status. I'll take a root beer, though."

"Sure, Johnny. Say, maybe you can tell me why our transportation base is suddenly buzzing with your fighters? You even got to show off that rocket plane you're testing. It's nice to see you guys, but what's up?"

"It's the Middle East. I guess they want our fighters close by just in case. As for me, this experimental plane is about to begin test-firing at targets from above the atmosphere, but say, I get a week off after tomorrow's mission. My fiancée, parents, and even my sister Maggie are flying out here. Maybe you could join us and show us around."

A woman soldier sitting next to David tapped him on the shoulder and pointed to the TV screen over the bar. "Hey, something's happening. Look, they stopped the game and put on a news bulletin."

The bartender flipped on the sound as the announcer spoke: "This is a Fox News Alert. All morning, we have been reporting a military buildup along the Israeli border from the Iranian Caliphate in the south and the Islamic State in the north. Rockets fired from both sides may have disabled Israel's defense system. Israeli fighters are bombing Islamic positions despite counter attacks by Iranian war planes.

"Our President's call for diplomacy has gone unheeded. We now have an unconfirmed report of a large missile launched toward Israel from Iran and shot down over Jordan. Iranian State TV denies the report and claims Israel launched the missile. They are showing videos of injured women and children casualties in Jordan. Stand by."

John said, "Does that answer your question about the fighter planes?"

"What's the point, John? Despite our paper commitment, our president won't send our troops to defend Israel. Maybe he'll send two sorties a day to blow up something for show, but he'll keep ordering us to avoid collateral damage, right?"

"My pilot friends in Turkey tell me they get a hundred 'stand down orders' for every 'go' order. I don't think anyone cares if the Holy Land becomes toast."

"God does. He'll protect them somehow, Johnny."

"Maybe, but it looks like our prayers and His promise will be the only help they'll get."

"Exactly, but that's all Israel's ever needed."

Suddenly, the lights began to go on and off, and the PA announced: "Now hear this. All military personnel to the flight line briefing room ASAP."

The message kept repeating. David and John gave each other gritted-teeth grins. Together they said, "Oh, oh."

FORTY

At the briefing, MPs were separating the flight crew officers and NCOs into one room and everyone else into another. Urgency was palpable. David and John quickly found two seats. Looking up, they faced the Base Commander on the podium flanked by two generals.

David whispered to John, "The Guy on the left is the Air Force Operations chief. Don't recognize the two-star. Must be from the Pentagon."

Without an introduction, the AFO chief stepped forward with the microphone. "I am General Silban, in charge of operations. General Dunfrey and I have just arrived from Washington. This briefing is confidential and will not be discussed outside this room. Understood?" Quiet followed. David hummed a squeaky "Uh, huh," without moving his lips.

"As everyone knows, the Islamic State on Israel's north and the greater Iranian Caliphate on her south are massing armies for an attack. Their short-range rockets are accurate these days, and we believe hundreds were launched and directed at Israeli missile defense. Both the Shiites and the

Sunnis want to be the first ones to get credit for Israel's destruction.

"Everyone is aware that the USS Carl Vincent is in the Gulf to protect Kuwait, and one news station leaked that USS Ronald Reagan is in the Mediterranean. That is correct. Iran launched a medium-range missile toward Tel Aviv. Be aware that this was a *nuclear* warhead, but it was destroyed over Jordan." Audience applause.

Silban paused again and let out a breath. "Here is what is *not* known outside of military intelligence. The Reagan was ordered to observe only and otherwise stand down, but *they* were the ones who intercepted and destroyed the missile with our newly updated Aegis Ashore missile defender."

Renewed applause spread in the room, but Dunfrey stepped up. "Hold on. The problem is that in saving Tel Aviv, they violated our president's stand-down order. Israel has been pleading for our help, and now they are desperate. To make matters worse, a Marine troop ship is now unloading about five thousand Marines and two Seal teams. They are joining IDF soldiers and, of course, Israel assumes we sent them. Also, Navy fighters from the Reagan have joined Israel in bombing the invading forces."

The room was filled with cheers and applause, but the generals motioned for quiet. Silban said, "You *do* realize that this is unprecedented and a breach of orders from the White

House. The Reagan has gone rogue, leaving the Administration in a political bind. Should they confirm or deny that this critical, life-saving support of our ally was authorized?"

Dunfrey added, "Secretary of the Navy, Westmore, was fired this morning by the president, and each of his three named successors quit when asked to replace him."

Silban leaned into the mike. "The Carl Vincent has launched cruise missiles and fighters as well. All of our vessels involved are not responding to communication from Central Command. This brings us to your mission. You are all being sent to our bases in Italy, Turkey, and Qatar and will stand ready for orders when you get there. You will pick up your initial flight orders today and begin departure at zero fourteen hundred hours."

The room became silent. "I have *one* question to ask of you before you leave, but first, I want you to bow your heads. You may meditate or pray as you wish." He waited a full half a minute before he spoke again. "Keep your heads bowed so that your comrades cannot tell who raises their hands in the affirmative. Should our president order you to attack our naval ships, would you obey those orders?"

After another quiet moment, he said, "Raise your heads. You should rejoice in being unanimous." Those on the podium applauded the troops.

Dunfrey took the microphone. "We salute you. Now I'm going to say something that could get me court-martialled. May the Lord be with you and may He save the Holy Land. God bless America. Dismissed."

The flight crews began to huddle around the sergeant who was calling out names and passing out orders. A Master Sergeant burst in the side door by the dais and rushed to the generals. They conferred a moment, and Silban returned to the podium, raising an arm overhead. "Attention! No one leaves just yet."

Dunfrey came up behind him and whispered something in his ear, to which he nodded. "Our country has just suffered a massive cyber attack likely from Iran. All our long-range missile defense systems are down at this moment. Our experts are working to restore readiness, but we do not know how long that will take." The Base Commander said something to him, and he held up a hand to the audience.

"The basic orders you have in your hand need not be changed, but the *route* you take to your bases *will* change. Here are your supplemental verbal orders." He wrote something on the paper before him, and the other general nodded.

"Pentagon states Iran does not have ICBMs, but a shorter-range nuke might come from a ship at sea. Your three squadrons will separate and follow search pattern theta, departure ASAP. You will be looking for any vessels at sea that might have missile-launching capabilities."

Dunfrey leaned into the microphone. "All of you have been trained in this. Satellite data will be forwarded regarding all vessels in the Atlantic. Huddle with your squadron leaders for any questions. Best of luck, gentlemen, and God be with you."

When all the orders had been handed out, John remained empty-handed. The sergeant said his orders must not have been changed, but pointed him to the squadron leader, Colonel Jones. "Colonel, Sir," He saluted. "We seem to be on a war footing now. Am I really supposed to just do another test run in the rocket plane? Sir, I'd like to take a fighter into battle if I may."

Jones had the appearance of a prizefighter, save for his bushy blonde mustache. "You may be one of our best pilots, Johnny, but you're staying with the test plane. It's even more critical now. Today it has full armament and it could be over any enemy vessel in a third the time of a fighter jet. We have set out a target barge in the mid Atlantic. You will fire on it from above the atmosphere as planned. However, there is a possibility these orders may change and you might end up with a real target. Understood?

"Yes, sir."

"So go to Hangar J and suit up as planned. Any questions?"

He saluted. "No questions, Sir."

FORTY-ONE

Two flight line Airmen helped John get into his special gear, actually a special, slimmed down space suit. *I wonder if those geniuses who want this rocket over a target so fast ever considered it takes twice as long for the pilot to get ready.*

The experimental plane was longer and sleeker than the jet fighters. It had two rocket drives in the tail, and small rotatable attitude jets on its wing tips. The plane also had conventional jet engines under each wing. When John had climbed the ladder to the cockpit, a crewman had to help him into the pilot seat and plug in the hoses and wires going to his suit. Still others worked on getting the craft fueled with both rocket and jet fuel. He looked at the empty copilot seat next to him and chuckled. *No sense in risking the lives of two test pilots, huh?*

One man on the ground crew tapped another on the shoulder and pointed to the cockpit. "I'm new on your crew. What's the pilot doing? Hope he's not sick, is he?"

"Nah, Captain Wright does that before every mission."

"He's bent over. Some sort of preflight routine?"

"Sort of. He's praying." He turned to the other Airman. "Ready? Time to pull this plane out of the hanger and fire it up."

Out on the runway, the last of the jet fighters were taking off as John started the conventional jet engines. *Hope Alicia and my family made it here. Sure would like to see them, but for now, I guess I'll have some fun popping a few barges.*

FORTY-TWO

"Hello, I'm Eric, Air Force Public Relations. Welcome to our VIP observation deck." He shook hands with John's parents. "I recognize you as Doctor Samuel Wright, and you must be his mother, Jasmine." Smiles and nods.

He turned to two other women. "And one of you ladies is his sister and the other his fiancée." He chuckled. "Don't want to guess."

One shook his hand. "I'm Maggie, the sister." She put her hand on a smiling, short-haired brunette beside her. "The beautiful one is my future sister-in-law, Alicia."

"Wonderful. So glad to have you all. This *should be* the final test of our new rocket plane, which we call Project Space Drop. Of course, if your boy misses the target, we'll have to keep trying until we get it right." More chuckling.

Eric gestured to seats along an expansive window. "He will be leaving an hour earlier than our original schedule, so you'll see him take off shortly. There's coffee, snacks, and drinks over there, and some Air Force history books on the other wall. Relax and call me on this phone if you need anything."

Alicia asked, "How will we know what is going on?"

"Good question. Before I go, I'll turn on the audio system so you can hear the control tower and general announcements as well. Unfortunately, we do not broadcast our communications with test pilots since they are confidential." He grinned and left.

Alicia turned to the others with gritted teeth. "I might as well confess right now. I'm going to be a lousy Air Force wife. I'm scared silly."

Jasmine gave her a hug. "Not to worry. I think all the wives are."

"But, Mrs. Wright, there's a Middle East crisis, and Johnny is doing stuff no one has ever done before."

"Puh-*leeze* call me Jazzy. We all worry about that boy, me more than most, but he has a very special talent when it comes to flying."

Maggie giggled. "Yeah, since about age six. He told me he often heard a voice in his head saying, 'Let's fly.' Remember when he launched off the second-floor balcony with homemade wings?"

Jasmine frowned at her. "Maggie, don't."

"Johnny had me help him balance on the rail before he jumped off."

"Maggie!"

"Oh, but he was all right. Skinned his arm, but he glided his home-made wings all the way to the fence."

Alicia giggled. "Oh thanks for that, Maggie. I feel so much better now."

"He's been my big brother hero ever since."

Alicia smiled at Samuel. "But *you* set him straight on the crazy stuff, huh, Dad?"

"Darn right. I taught him about engineering and preplanning. He didn't imagine his landing area. With my help the next time he made it *over* the fence, another twenty yards and landed on his feet besides. Jazzy was a little upset at this, but when he was thirteen, he joined a hang-gliding club."

Jasmine moved between them. "All right. Enough for now, both of you. Maybe this could wait until Johnny's back for dinner." Alicia nodded, her teeth in a gritty smile.

The speaker announced: "Fighter twenty-two delta cleared for takeoff."

Samuel motioned to the soft chairs by the window. "Okay, guys, best you believe our boy's going to be just fine. Let's just settle in, relax, and watch the show."

FORTY-THREE

The plane's jet engines powered him up to forty thousand feet at a forty-five-degree angle. John called ground control. "Forty thousand. All systems normal. Switching to rocket."

"Roger. Maintain heading zero one two. Climb to eight five thousand and hold."

"Roger, wilco."

John shut down the jets and hit the rocket drive that squashed him back into the seat at five g's. *Ugg, you'd think I'd get used to this.*

The "flat" Earth became a huge blue and white ball below, and the "sky" turned black. "Level at eighty-five. Proceeding to coordinates."

"Roger. Activate scanning radar and report."

"I have one vessel below and slightly north."

"That should be USS-41. She's your rescue ship if you need one, so please don't blow her up."

John laughed. "Hey, behind me, I identify our squadron down at thirty thousand coming this way. Looks like I got way ahead of everyone."

"That *is* the idea, John. All right, proceed to…hold on…hold on…John, there is a general emergency bulletin. I'm putting it through."

Another voice came on his earphones. "Attention, attention, all military personnel on emergency frequency and all ships at sea. Satellite confirms the launch of an ICBM from Iran, preliminary data indicates the target to be mid North America. This is not an exercise. Stand by."

"Ground control back, John. This is no joke. Our present mission is aborted. You are advised to proceed to Lakenheath Air Base, Scotland. All air and ground traffic is directed away from East Coast cities."

"This is the ICBM that they're not supposed to have, right?"

"And launched, I presume, from the area we were never allowed to inspect."

"Totally horrible. I assume our administration will condemn the destruction of America in the strongest diplomatic terms."

"If they survive. John, I'll stay on this frequency but switch to your emergency radio and listen to the updates. You may not have enough rocket fuel to make Scotland, but the jets will take you the rest of the way. Remember, your navigating computer is voice-activated. Good luck."

"I wish *you* good luck." *And I wish I could find all this unbelievable, but unfortunately, it makes macabre sense. Iran's Ayatollah had this planned all along, just waiting for any excuse.* He turned on his long-range scanning radar to the east. *And, sure enough, there it is. All the pure evil of this world headed our way.*

The emergency radio announced, "Update. Our missile defense systems remain offline. The target area is calculated to be New York City, with an impact in 17.5 minutes. Civilians are now advised to take cover in their homes and offices. All pedestrians are advised to get into the subway system. Stand by."

Crap. We're helpless. John's bright blue eyes snapped wide open, and he slapped the side of his helmet. *Boing! Wait, maybe not.*

"Computer, target is on radar at ninety-two thousand feet. Calculate interception course."

"Telemetry data on speed required. Unable to comply at this time."

That sucker is getting here fast. "Estimate time of compliance."

"Twenty-nine seconds."

Plenty of time to change your mind. John, what do you think you're doing?

"Calculation complete. Rendezvous or intercept?"

"Rendezvous. Commence navigation."

With his hands off the controls, the attitude jets swung the craft around, facing west. Suddenly, full rocket power came on, and John's G-suit inflated to keep him conscious. Ground control said, "Hey, John, you're headed the wrong way."

"Not if I'm gonna take a shot at this thing."

"That's crazy, but look, if you try it, keep ten miles away. It's full of rocket fuel and standard explosives as well. I'm signing off. We nonessentials are all headed for the bunkers. God help us."

John felt the rocket engines backing off. He looked out to see his ship approaching the huge missile and pulling alongside. *My God, this thing's a monster.*

He swiveled with the attitude jets to face it and checked the rocket fuel gauge. *Run' in on empty. Crap.* He began to maneuver away to get distance from the missile but saw the nose cone warhead dividing into three sections. Suddenly, his rocket engines quit, and he began to drop away.

Immediately, John fired both his torpedoes at the missile. A horrendous explosion resulted. He and his crushed plane were swatted away like a home run baseball. Spinning wildly, the plane and its unconscious pilot began to plunge from ninety thousand feet to the ocean below.

FORTY-FOUR

Samuel threw out the question to anyone. "Who here believes this story about a threatened missile attack?" Their group had been moved to a basement storage room where they sat in folding chairs against shelves full of groceries.

Maggie shrugged. "Well, Dad, there must be *some* kind of terrorist threat out there. They're taking it seriously."

Jasmine said, "At least we're still VIPs. The base personnel are in the gym, and we're sitting here with enough food to feed an army."

"Well, of course," Maggie gestured to the walls. "It *is* food for the army."

"Could it be there's really a war going on and it's secret," Alicia intoned, her voice squeaking like an old shoe. "Maybe Johnny and all those others are going into *battle*."

Maggie got up and put an arm around Alicia's shoulders. "Let's not put the worst spin on it. Yes, all the planes are going to the Middle East, but Johnny's just doing a test flight in a plane he's flown half a dozen times already."

"That doesn't explain squirreling everyone below ground, though. Does it?"

"No, but that cute guy Eric promised me he'd be back as soon as he knew anything more."

Alicia's eyes flared. "We could all be dead in a minute, and you're thinking about cute guy Eric?"

Jasmine wiggled her hands in the air. "All right girls, we're all feeling tense. Let's say a prayer for Johnny and our country. Pray for heavenly intervention."

After Jasmine's prayer she said, "I hope we're all feeling a bit better, and I notice there's a box of chocolate chips on the top shelf in case…"

Eric entered swiftly, his expression grim. "Please have a seat. General Silban asked me to brief you on the truth about what has been going on. While this will shortly be public information, it is still classified, understood? No cell phones, please."

Heads nodded. "Iran launched a nuclear ICBM at us after first disabling our missile defense with a cyber attack."

Eric responded to the horrified moans. "But there is no danger at the moment and the all clear will sound shortly. The ballistic missile had a Russian-made, three-part warhead targeting Washington, New York, and Boston. It was mostly destroyed twenty minutes ago, but the one for Boston was only damaged and is heading for the North Atlantic. No threat to us except a tidal surge."

Eric waited for this to sink in. Samuel inquired, "But if we had no missile defense, how was it destroyed? Do we have a killer satellite?"

"I wish. No, the good news is your son destroyed it in the XR-5."

"Johnny? Our Johnny shot it down?"

"Chased it, shot it, killed it. Totally amazing. We didn't think that was possible. But the bad news is, he did this at close range. I'm sorry, but the explosion hit the XR-5 as well. We lost his transponder signal and all communication."

Alicia screeched and began to weep into her hands. Samuel said, "But you don't know for *sure* his plane is down."

"No, but satellite imagery was obscured by the fireball, and frankly, we were all trying to follow that live warhead. I wish I could give you more encouraging news. We have a search vessel in the area and two helicopters out looking."

Jasmine said flatly, "My son is all right. I just feel it."

Eric offered a slim smile. "We all hope so, but whatever the outcome, know this. Your son just saved one hundred million people and his country."

FORTY-FIVE

John snapped into consciousness with a searing pain in his right shoulder and the half-ball of blue earth tumbling wildly outside his cracked-open cockpit canopy. Instinctively, he reached for the pilot eject lever, but a hand covered his. "Better not. The system is damaged, and it would likely kill you."

He looked to his right and faced an angel man sitting on his wings with blond, curly hair and a grin. The angel said. "I'm Andrew. Do you suppose you could use the attitude jets to stop the spinning before we both get dizzy?"

John began to struggle with the wingtip jets and his shoulder pain. "So, mother's story wasn't a fairy tale. You're my guardian, huh? Am I dead?"

"Right on the first count, Captain. Negative on the second. You're alive. There, we're smoothing out. Nice job.

"Alive sounds like a maybe. Anything else you can tell me?"

"You should know, your right wing's bent back, its engine is full of debris, and the tank on that side is leaking fuel. I opened the stuck wheel well door for you on my way in, but the gear won't come down all the way."

"Thanks, Andrew, but since we're in free fall, and the one jet I have won't work in space, it looks like burning up and crashing is about a minute into my future."

"Unless what?"

"Oh, great, a pop quiz just before I die. Unless I pray?"

Andrew laughed. "Well, that's always a good idea, but *while* you pray, Captain, think of what else you can do to save your plane?"

"One engine left. Feather the right one. Try and start the left one as we hit atmosphere." John hit the starter. Nothing.

"Angle down a bit to get some air in, John. Careful, too much speed and turbulence could tear off that right wing."

He hit it again, and the jet engine whined into life. "Hallelujah." The craft bounced up with a creaking sound in the wing and settled again, heading slightly down.

"Why are you doing that, John?"

"I'm skipping on the top of the atmosphere to lose some speed. Here we go again."

"Hey, good. That's working."

"Okay, now I'm pulling the flaps slowly. I'd like to keep us going at ninety miles an hour in slow flight, but all the instruments are out. Suggestions, Andrew?"

"Yeah, first pull all your fuel from the crumpled right tank. It's leaking pretty fast. Also, cut off all the power switches to your panel."

"Thanks. I get it. If anything *doesn't* have a short, it will stay on when I reboot. Do you think I can make it back to shore? I'd hate to ditch into the ocean."

The plane continued a slow descent, and the waves became visible. "Really don't know, John. It depends on how fast the leak is. You're about nine hundred miles out, and ditching could be problematic. The canopy's frozen in position, and it's only cracked open eight inches."

"So, I'll drown. I get it. And you were starting to cheer me up, too. What's that in your hand? A knife?"

Andrew held up a jagged piece of metal. "Oh, this was embedded in your shoulder. I took it out while you were unconscious and stopped the bleeding." He tossed it on the floor. "Just concentrate on all you can do to save fuel."

John leveled the plane a few hundred feet above the ocean. "This poor plane sure doesn't handle the way it should. Only two panel systems stayed on: the tower radio and the navigation beacon reception. My plan is to fly slowly and at low altitude all the way. Also, I'll see if I can't get my suit off in case I have to ditch. Maybe I can get through the crack if I have to."

Andrew gave John a reassuring grin. "Should give you a fighting chance." He disconnected the tubes for space travel and undid part of John's suit.

John winced as his arm pulled out of the sleeve. "Ouch. Okay, it's free."

"All right, Johnny, time for me to get out of this dimension. Besides, I'm adding weight by staying here. You're my boy, and I'll be praying you make it. God loves you big time, John. Me too."

"Can't thank you enough, Andy. I'm gonna give you a hug." After a clumsy one-armed, one-wing hug attempt, John asked, "Will you come back for me if I die?"

"Sure, but I hope that will be at least seventy years from now. Say, when I leave, pull out the emergency kit under your seat so it will be handy. Oh, and by the way, Heaven and Earth really appreciate your saving a few million lives. God be with you."

A swirling portal appeared in the side of the plane. Andrew gave him a grin and a fist bump, slipped into the vortex, and was gone.

John was alone with the sound of his lone engine. It sputtered, and he switched the fuel supply to the remaining tank just in time.

John pulled out the emergency kit and began to struggle with the rest of his suit despite the pain in his shoulder. *Sure sounds like I'll be drowning in this cockpit soon, and Andy just didn't want to tell me.* He flicked a few switches. *No working lights left except my right wing tip, and even if I do make shore, it's gonna be nighttime.*

FORTY-SIX

John's family had been moved to a two-bedroom hotel suite nearby pending the results of the recovery operations. They all sat in the living area watching the TV news. Alicia had wrapped herself in a blanket with only her red-eyed face showing. Jasmine spoke in a soft voice, "Alicia, Dear, we're going to bed. We've heard the war news twice now, and the base will call us if they have any updates on Johnny."

"I'll put the volume down, Mrs. Wri—I mean Jazzy." She pulled a tissue from the box nearby and blew her nose. "I don't think I can sleep."

"I understand, but I'm sure he's all right. I got some milk and cookies from the hotel. They're on your bedside table and should help you sleep when you're ready."

Maggie lay on the couch, her head against Alicia, but she sat up. "Okay, I'll get the cookies, but I'm sticking here with Alicia."

Jasmine smiled. "All right, you two, but I keep telling you: I'm sure Johnny's okay."

Maggie came back with the cookies as her parents closed the bedroom door. "I have to tell you, Alicia, my mom has some special connection with God. If she says Johnny's okay, I'm sure he is."

Alicia slipped out of her blanket and hugged Maggie. "Oh, I pray you are right, but even if you don't become my sister in law, I hope you'll always be my friend."

Maggie pouted at her. "Always, and I'm keeping you for a sister, too." She flipped off the TV mute button. "The news is back on."

"Breaking News Alert: The United States has officially joined the French alliance in declaring war on Iran and the Islamic State. Egypt and Saudi Arabia are participating as well. We have William Tucker in Jerusalem on the line. What's the current status, Bill?"

"Cynthia, from where I'm standing, I can hear explosions every few seconds. Allied and Israeli forces are decimating the invading armies. I have reports that Iran no longer has an Air Force. Bunker-busting bombs continue to destroy their nuclear facilities and…wait." He bent over, listening to his earpiece, then looked back up at the camera. "This just in. "Our fighters discovered a second nuclear missile in the very process of being launched in Iran, and they destroyed it. Hopefully, we'll have a video later."

"Well, Bill, there are rumors that the nuclear explosion eight hundred miles northeast of Boston was a long-range Iranian ICBM. Any confirmation on that?"

"Not from here, Cynthia."

Her face filled the screen. "Thank you, Bill. There is no scheduled White House briefing at this time, but we will continue to try and get a Pentagon spokesperson to talk to us. We'll be back after this."

Maggie flipped the mute back on as the ad began. "Seems we know more about that missile than the press. Come on to bed. I'll give you a neck rub."

FORTY-SEVEN

Dover Air Controllers, Matt and Jim, sat at their consoles chatting. "Quiet night considering, huh, Jim."

"Yeah, well, most of our aircraft are overseas. Too bad they cancelled the Orioles game." He yawned. "Hey, wait. It looks like the transport from Wright Patterson is coming into our control space."

The speaker announced: "This is transport Charlie Alpha twenty-one, west of Dover, requesting landing instructions."

"Uh, Charlie Alpha, enter pattern north, and turn right to runway one niner five. No other traffic. Over."

"Roger, Dover."

Matt turned to Jim. "Our relief takes over in an hour. You wanna hit Sam's bar and find out from the media what they're not telling us about the war news?"

"Thanks, but my boy's got batting practice at nine tomorrow and I'm sleepy already."

Static came on the speaker along with a faint, garbled voice. "Shhh-five- off coast- shhh- emerg-shhh."

Matt said, "That's probably for Washington International. Sometimes they're too close to us. You make out what they said?"

The speaker said, "Charlie Alpha turning for final approach. Over."

"Clear to land, Charlie Alpha. Over."

"This-shhh-XR-5 requesting emergency landing at Dover. shhh-Do you read?"

Matt and Jim gave each other white eyeballs and gasped. "Rocket XR-5, good to hear you! Wow!" Matt said, "Can you fly pattern? Over."

"Uh, negative. I'm on fumes and damaged. Require straight in emergency landing."

Matt pointed at Jim, who was already hitting the alert for emergency crews. "You got it, XR-5. Use zero one fiver. Slight tailwind. Help on the way. Over."

Jim pointed up with a wiggling finger. Matt remembered the other plane and slapped his forehead. "Charlie Alpha: abort landing. Emergency arrival on zero one fiver. Over."

"Roger that, Dover."

The men strained to see out their window. Sirens and flashing red lights were heading out on the runway. "Can't see a thing."

"Wait, there he is. He's got no lights."

The crippled XR-5 crossed the runway edge, crabbing in sideways before its remaining engine quit. John straightened it a bit as the plane bounced into contact. One wheel was only halfway down, and on the second bounce, the wing hit with a squealing trail of sparks.

The plane slid sideways down the runway, finally coming to a stop near the fire engines. With practiced precision, the rescue team drove up, put a ladder to the twisted canopy cover, and the first man looked in. "Hi," John said. "Sorry I banged up the car, Dad. Hope it's insured."

Rescue man laughed. "It'll come out of your paycheck. How are you doing in there?"

"Shoulder injury, otherwise okay. No fire worries. All the fuel's out."

The man tried to lift the canopy and called to others on the ground. "We'll need the jaws to pry this off." He looked back inside. "How's it feel to be a national hero?"

"I'll settle for being Alicia's hero and alive. What happened to the third warhead?"

The men had the jaw device in position, and the canopy yielded with crunks and snaps. "You don't know? The third one fell into the sea. It detonated, but way away from land. No casualties."

John began to crawl out, wincing with pain. "Thanks be to God."

FORTY-EIGHT

Alicia was the first to the phone when it rang at two AM. Her shriek got Jasmine and Samuel staggering out of their bedroom. "He's alive! He landed. He's alive!"

She bounced around before putting the phone back to her ear. "Sorry, are you still there? Uh huh, uh huh."
She put the phone down and faced the family with a shekinah-like glow on her happy face. "He's in the base infirmary, minor injury to his shoulder. He wants to see us, of course." She did a few more bounces. "Eric is coming with the van."

Jasmine held up her hands with a "you see?" gesture. Alicia embraced her. "You never doubted, did you?"

"Nope. Johnny keeps coming back from his adventures with his favorite saying: 'No big deal, Mom,' so I'm used to this."

Samuel said, "Huh, well, this was a bit of an extreme big deal, Jazzy. Let's all get some traveling clothes on."

When Eric came to their door, all were ready except Alicia, who was working on her hair and makeup. When they pulled up to the little hospital, Eric told them, "You do know that visiting like this is totally against the hospital rules, but the Base Commander said, 'whatever Johnny wants,' so here we are."

John was sitting up in bed with his right shoulder bandaged and a Cheshire Cat grin. Alicia jumped on top of the bed, and the kissing began. "Ouch," he said. "Careful with the arm."

"Oh, darling, they made it sound like it was all over, like there was no way you could have survived."

John swung his legs over to sit on the edge of the bed. Jasmine gave him a squeeze and a cheek kiss. He pointed to her. "I owe you an apology, Mom. I never really believed your angel stories, but I just met Andrew."

"Tsk, tsk. And we showed you the pictures and everything. Did he help you fly the airplane?"

"Not exactly, but he dropped in and stopped me from making fatal mistakes. I was too close to the Iranian missile when I blew it up, so it damaged the XR-5. He stopped me from pulling the broken pilot eject and told me about the fuel leak. Andrew said he was able to help 'cause of all your prayers."

Alicia was draped over his good shoulder. She rolled her eyes toward him. "And you'll never stop getting *those*, my darling." That got another kiss.

FORTY-NINE

Two weeks later, the President and the Speaker of the House presented John with the Congressional Medal of Honor in the Rose Garden. Alicia and his family looked on from front row seats. As the President pinned it on John's dress blues, he proclaimed, "John Andrew Wright, now Major, United States Air Force, this is a token from a grateful nation."

The First Lady sat next to Jasmine, who was wearing her hair in an uncharacteristically well-mannered trim and wearing a beatific smile. Beside her, of course, was his dad, Samuel, showing a proud thumbs up, and Alicia blowing air kisses. Maggie sat on the end texting on her phone.

The President took the podium. "Major Wright's heroic action is unprecedented in its historical meaning for our country, and we will never know how many millions of lives he saved. I asked him if there was anything he would want in return from the United States. He asked for ten minutes of uncensored airtime. I told him I guess we could settle for that." A murmur of chuckles spread around the audience.

The President stepped aside, gesturing to John who moved to the podium with a grin. The audience became quiet. John adjusted his arm sling and thought. *Uh, oh, now I wish I had written this out. Mom always said just to let the Holy Spirit help with the hard parts.*

"Hello everyone. I'm a lot more comfortable in a fighter jet than public speaking, so please give me some slack." He spotted "Aunt" Paula with Steve, sitting with his buddy David in the crowd. David stuck out his tongue at him, and he felt better right away.

"The first thing I want to say before anyone makes too much of what I did is to tell you that everyone I've ever met in this army of ours would have done exactly the same thing I did, given the opportunity; maybe even my friend, Dave." David was slowly nodding "no" with pursed lips. That made him laugh.

John's words became measured. "Both Israel and America were dedicated to the one true God at their inception, and as long as our countries remain faithful to Him, we remain under His protection. The story of Israel in the Bible is a lesson to us about how our countries fare with and without that protection. I recommend that each one of you take time to study the true and inspired word of God."

A few in the audience suddenly found the scenery more interesting, but most were attentive, even Maggie. "For thousands of years, even people who know God have preferred to create their own religions and rules. Not only does this turn off the unbeliever who sees us as arrogant hypocrites, but it covers up God's true desire to place righteousness in our hearts and simply abide with us."

"There is a serious battle going on for the hearts of men and women. This battle is not just waged on Earth, but in Heaven. Those nuclear warheads were sent by men whose spirits are captured by Satan, whose plan is to destroy all humans who worship the one true God. I am asking you now to pray for those men, not for their desires, but that they may see truth and save their eternal souls."

John took a deep breath and smiled at the people. "All scientists search for the truth, and they know there cannot be multiple contradicting truths. I proclaim that one's personal salvation, as well as the salvation of our entire civilization, depends on faith in Jesus Christ. He is the *only* way for us. He is the way of truth and life, eternal life."

"Our founding fathers were devout Christians, and John Adams said our Nation's principles are the general principles of Christianity, and Dwight D. Eisenhower said 'Without God there could be no American form of government.'" He looked over a hushed audience. "My favorite, though, is Ronald Reagan. He said 'If we ever forget that we are one nation under God, we will be one nation gone under.'"

"I know this is sounding more like a sermon, but I want you to know how deeply God cares about each and every one of you. My mother and I came within a whisker of death once, but thanks to God and His anointed helpers, I stand here today. One of his helpers was an angel named Andrew." A grin spread across his face. "Don't know how he does it, but every year Andrew sends my mom a Mother's Day card.

"Please know that I was not alone in preventing this nuclear annihilation. I was following God's plan even if I didn't understand it. I am just one of many who serve Him to protect this nation and our country, dedicated to God."

John looked up and closed his eyes. *Thank you for these words, Lord.*

"All of us in America have been granted a second chance. My prayer today is this: may each and every one of us use this chance to draw close to God, rededicate ourselves, and in so doing, get on the right path again."

Pascal John Imperato began writing Fiction in Junior High, became a High School literary editor, and continued writing short stories in Creative Writing classes at Johns Hopkins University. Getting a Medical Degree at Duke University and beginning a Pennsylvania practice temporarily resulted in scientific and journal writing. After a born-again revelation, he resumed fiction writing once more, but with a messianic twist under the pen name of "John Pascal." He has published "The Revelation Trilogy," comprised of three novels: "The Bee," "Domes," and "2248." "PRISONER 1171" was published in 2014. "WINGIN' IT," released in 2015, is a prequel to "My Child."

Pascal lives and writes in Southern California.

ACKNOWLEDGEMENTS: The author is grateful for the suggestions received from dedicated employees of Deeper Still and the Fallbrook Pregnancy Counseling Center. No endorsement is requested or implied. Also appreciated is the help and advice of the San Diego Christian Writers' Guild and its Temecula Critique Group, hosted by Rebecca Farnbach.

www.ingramcontent.com/pod-product-compliance
Lightning Source LLC
Chambersburg PA
CBHW022159170626
46807CB00005B/2271